Praise for *The Vietri Project*

"Deft, masterly storytelling . . . this complex, substantive debut offers a singular and transfixing take on the nature of identity—both national and personal—and the dangers of secrecy, both national and personal. And, of course, what it means to come of age in a broken world, a world that has been broken for generations."   —*New York Times*

"Nicola DeRobertis-Theye has written a smart, taut debut about a woman in her twenties trying to find a path into the rest of her life. *The Vietri Project* is a riveting, shifting quest, an evocative trip to Rome, and a beautiful portrayal of the ways you need to return to the past in order to move forward. A great delight from start to finish."

—Lily King, *New York Times* bestselling author
of *Writers and Lovers*

"*The Vietri Project* offers the best kind of mystery, one where each new discovery not only opens up our understanding of the story but also of the world we live in. Nicola DeRobertis-Theye writes with precision, such finely tuned sentences, and conjures the past without getting lost in it, using it as a map to find a way towards something beautiful."

—Kevin Wilson, author of *New York Times*
bestseller *Nothing to See Here*

The Vietri Project

The Vietri Project

A NOVEL

Nicola DeRobertis-Theye

HARPER PERENNIAL

NEW YORK • LONDON • TORONTO • SYDNEY • NEW DELHI • AUCKLAND

HARPER ● PERENNIAL

This is a work of fiction. Names, characters, places, and incidents are products of the author's imagination or are used fictitiously and are not to be construed as real. Any resemblance to actual events, locales, organizations, or persons, living or dead, is entirely coincidental.

A hardcover edition of this book was published in 2021 by HarperCollins Publishers.

FIRST HARPER PERENNIAL EDITION PUBLISHED 2022.

Designed by Leah Carlson-Stanisic

Library of Congress Cataloging-in-Publication Data has been applied for.

ISBN 978-0-06-301771-9 (pbk.)

22 23 24 25 26   LSC   10 9 8 7 6 5 4 3 2 1

To University Press Books, Berkeley

The Vietri Project

Chapter One

I first heard of signor Vietri while working in a small bookstore in Berkeley specializing in the university and other scholarly presses, which endured somehow through the early years of the Amazon empire despite its retreating margins and slowly capitulating customer base. I was in my last year of college, living in a small box of a room that I was compelled to enter through my roommate's bedroom, eyes averted. Before the bookstore I'd been working at an upscale Italian deli and import store on Claremont Avenue, where I believed the deciding factor in my hiring had been my ability to confidently pronounce the word tagliatelle. After a year of arranging pesto mayo on ciabatta and gagging at the white ooze of mortadella on the meat slicer, I'd applied to the bookstore, which had given me shifts on Saturdays and Wednesday nights.

Soon after I was hired, a letter had arrived with a list of over fifty books that a Giordano Vietri, in Rome, was hoping we could track down and ship to him. Requests like these weren't infrequent for our store, but Vietri's order was unusual in its volume. Because I was the newest staff member, "the Vietri Project," as we called it, was given to me. The list of books, which included the city of publication as well as the year, was full of misspellings and typos of both the titles and authors' names. I suspected it had been written on a typewriter, because what word processing program would not have corrected the frequent spaces missing between words? I ran my fingers over the back of the paper to feel for the faint bumps I thought a typewriter might leave, but the evidence remained inconclusive.

As the days went on, infused by the leisurely pace of the store, I began to pay closer attention to the books themselves. Some of the early titles that stood out to me were *Medicine, Rationality, and Experience*; *The Cultural Phenomenology of Charismatic Healing*; *Pain as Human Experience*; and *Patients and Healers in the Contexts of Culture*. I had the thought that these were the book purchases of a dying intellectual, but concluded that it was more likely that this signor Vietri was an anthropologist, who as a category bought the most eclectic books. I was an English major, but it was beginning to occur to me that, perhaps, everything was anthropology.

After a few weeks, when the books had arrived and been shipped off to Rome, that probably would have been the end of my thoughts of Vietri had not another letter arrived just eleven days later. This time the books requested had become more geographically specific: *Medicine in China*; *Mystical Dimensions of Islam*; *A Balinese Formula for Living*; *Mind and Experience in Tahiti*. In addition, the number of books requested had doubled. I assembled the order while trying surreptitiously to finish my honors thesis on Thomas Hardy at the front desk, thinking there was small chance signor Vietri had even received his first order of books, let alone had time to read any of them.

At this point, I imagined that he was founding some sort of library, perhaps for a small college. However, by the next list of requests, for *Early Sanskrit Scriptures*; *Hunting, Animism, and Personhood among the Siberian Yukag*; and *Death Ritual in Late Imperial China*, along with a string of books on Taoism and immortality, I began to construct the image in my head that was to remain my conception of the signore: that of an old man alone in a crumbling Roman apartment building, surrounded by hundreds of books not in his native language, frantically researching his own mortality.

I also had the opportunity to acquire clues of his existence from his letters. He ended one of his responses, "Please kindly do not refer to me as 'Professor,' as I am not." He always addressed his letters "Dear Sirs," though no letter had ever been answered by anyone other than a woman, one of the store's several female managers in their fifties, who would pass the work of researching and assembling the titles along to me. The letters began to arrive with more detailed instructions, he wanted only paperback editions, if available, and if not available the cloth edition should cost no more than fifty US dollars. So he wasn't working for a library, which would have taken only hardcovers. He insisted on paying by bank transfer, and agreed to pay all of the fees imposed by both the Italian and the American banks on either end. Every order came with an expiration date, six or seven months off, as if, though reading of immortality, he was keenly aware of his own body's temporal limitations.

The next books he ordered, around the time I graduated

and was making half-hearted attempts to apply for what I thought of as real jobs, were on ancient scriptures from China and the Indian subcontinent, studies of animism and alchemy. I had no luck with these work applications, few of my peers had either, that the economy was about to tip over seemed known to everyone except my graduating class. Instead I had moved in with my boyfriend to an apartment across the border in Oakland, and felt lucky when the store agreed to increase my hours to full-time. So I was the one who ordered for the signore, over the next two years, the Tibetan and Egyptian Books of the Dead, with commentaries, then books concerning spiritual possessions, relations between the living and the dead in island societies, shamanism. After the first year there was a return to books on healing, Navajo medicinal practices, Mexican folk remedies, unorthodox medicine in the West, the orders arriving regularly every few months, so that if Berkeley had experienced seasons I would have had the opportunity to mark them.

His final order before I left the store consisted almost entirely of books on oracles and divinations, meditation and self-actualization. Because I was at this point, and had been for more than a year, the only one placing and receiving Vietri's orders, packing the books, and shipping them off, I'd come to increasingly feel like he could be a creation of my imagination. The letters passed along to me and the heavy boxes in their international M-bags I wheeled to the post office seemed the only proofs of his existence.

✤ ✤ ✤

The signore's books were piled on a high shelf above our normal customer holds, and I had a habit of flipping through them at random, gathering a collection of facts that amassed in my memory. From them I learned that there is a plant whose leaves, when chewed, can soothe heart palpitations, and this plant produces a tiny red flower in the shape of a heart; that in shamanistic séances in Siberia infertile women were encouraged to mimic the sounds of a reindeer calf; that the sage who wrote the Ramayana was instructed to chant the word for death, mara, over and over, and after decades of saying Mara-MaraMaraMara realized he was intoning the name of god, RamaRamaRamaRama.

Business at the store had slowed. The economy had crashed three months after I'd graduated, and I viewed each day I spent there as improbable as the next. Sometimes a professor I'd had just a few years before would come into the store, but they never recognized me. Somehow two years had passed, and I remained, locking the building at eight o'clock on Friday and Saturday nights, the key heavy in my pocket as I biked home to the cheap apartment I shared with my boyfriend, occasionally spending weekends at home in Sacramento, where I'd grown up, stuck between two lives I didn't feel I'd chosen.

One day I looked up some numbers. We had sent Vietri over a thousand books during the course of the last two and a half years, and he had requested more than five hundred more.

Most of the latter category were out of print and unable to be ordered, but some of the texts I could find no records for anywhere in my research, though his list claimed they were relatively recent publications. He had paid us tens of thousands of dollars for the books, in addition to hundreds in shipping costs and bank fees, but still insisted no single volume exceed the cost of fifty dollars.

With these numbers, he could not possibly have had time to read even a small fraction of the books we were sending him. The time it took him to compile his lists of books to be ordered must have been extensive, but I assumed he had no assistant as I knew that all communications, even about the most trivial things, came from him, and always via letter. Surely if the books were for a library I would have found some sort of reference online, but when I had googled his name when we'd first begun receiving his orders I'd found only references to the town of Castel Giordano, near Vietri sul Mare, towns that I was surprised to see were not far from the one where my grandfather had been born.

But since then, Google Maps had added certain Italian cities to Street View, and one afternoon I realized I could search for where he lived. I did, after all, have the address where we shipped his books. I typed 147 via Bevanda, Roma, into the browser and was faced with the familiar oranges and beiges of Rome, a group of pale brick apartment buildings, balconies protruding in orderly rectangles, with well-tended plants overflowing them and satellite dishes on their sides rising above the graffiti. My mother had grown up in Rome, and I'd been sent for several summers in my early teens to stay with my aunts and cousins there, attempting to absorb this other family, this other city, but it had been years since I had been back.

That night, the image of Vietri's apartment building fresh in my mind, I described my curiosity about him to my boyfriend. I'd never mentioned the signore before, but seeing where he lived had loosened something around my idea of him, made it clear that he existed in our same world. I'd made a pasta for dinner, and we ate it at the coffee table, sitting on the floor, our backs against the couch. We'd never bothered to buy a dining room table.

He's probably just an academic doing research, my boyfriend said when I'd finished.

But he's so old . . . I trailed off. I had in mind a question about time, about futility, but the true words wouldn't arise.

How do you know he's old?

I hesitated, wondering if I had an answer. His handwriting, I said. His signature looks shaky. Plus, he doesn't use email.

My boyfriend shook his head and took another bite of the spaghetti, uncurious. I looked around, disappointed, and upset with myself for feeling this disappointment. Our apartment looked just like any of the ones I'd had in college, with its bland craigslisted couch, the ancient sponge in the sink. I was surprised, suddenly, to see how little I'd impressed myself on this life. I'd always felt a solidarity with this boyfriend, he worked in a tile kiln in West Berkeley and we were both witnessing the changes among our friends, who were moving to the city in order to commute to start-up jobs in the South Bay, or being promoted to manage restaurants that raised their own flocks of ducks, or else were attempting to postpone these decisions by applying to graduate school. We'd never talked about these changes, about the sense I had that we were becoming marooned by staying in the same place, and I appreciated this about him, content as we were with the free popcorn at the bar down the street, the occasional house parties we biked home from with red eyes and pleasantly murky minds. That night, however, a thought that had been shadowing me again arose with force, it was the knowledge that on my next birthday I would be twenty-five.

Soon after, that quiet life I'd lived with my boyfriend had built up in its quietness until I wanted to scream. While drunk, he'd begun to whisper things like I can't wait to marry you, and I would freeze, panicked, because even though our life together had given me a sense of comfort I'd never really known, there was a great uncertainty that hovered over me, and I knew I could never do that to another person, tie them to me before I knew my fate. I didn't want to re-create the family I'd come from. Books were the only thing I considered permanent, real, not the regular customers at the bookstore; not our friends, mostly my boyfriend's; not the apartment we shared, the sex we would have, our muffled orgasms. And so, though I loved my boyfriend in a quiet way, I began to research plane tickets, to read the Lonely Planets and the Rough Guides at work, to sleep, on occasional evenings, with a coworker, a poet with an apartment near the store. I would tell my boyfriend our evening events were running late, though really this coworker and I would steal a bottle of the cheap wine kept for readings and drink it on his mattress, alone on the floor of his studio, and if my boyfriend ever noticed that my hair was now wrapped on top of my head when before it had been loose and neatly combed, that I turned away more and more when his hand made its way through the slip between my underwear and the hair there, he never said anything, never reacted, so I took it for granted he must know something was going on, must suspect something, and I was not ready for the depth of the betrayal he felt, nor for his anger when I announced that I was leaving. He wouldn't believe me for days, he said he would travel with me, was on the verge of putting in notice at his job, and when I finally realized that he was serious, I told him about the nights on the coworker's mattress, told him about the things we'd done together that I'd sworn to my boyfriend I would only do with him, and only then did he believe me and let me go.

I thought of Vietri from time to time during those months of flight, as I tried my best to lose myself in various countries across South America, when I saw *The Tibetan Book of the Dead* in a fellow traveler's backpack, when a woman with few remaining teeth pushed me toward her offerings of dried llama fetuses, promising the cure for something as my Spanish eluded me. I thought of the books he had read, the things he must know, whereas the more I saw of the world during those months the less I felt I knew about it, and the image of his apartment on the via Bevanda became a beacon, glowing orange-beige, it was light-infused in my memory. Then suddenly I'd run out of beach islands in Bahia, was sick of refusing psychedelic mushrooms from Frenchmen a decade or two past the point when they should have been out every day in the sun, and I wondered where there was left to go. So that's how it happened that one afternoon I arrived at the Termini station in Rome, my body stiff from the overnight flight from Rio, the train ride from the airport, and I, thirsty in the August heat, went shamefaced to the McDonald's there and ordered a Coke Light, and, seeing the list on the menu board of bevande, thought that I might, as long as I was here, try to visit the apartment on the via Bevanda.

Chapter Two

The first thing about Rome was always the light, and then it was the people. There was a reaction of spaces and crowds, angles and shadows, that remained imprinted on my mind, the way its short structures, thin alleys would open to a wide avenue, another piazza, suddenly drawing the eye upwards. It had been ten years since I'd been in Rome, and in those previous summers I'd been driven around in tiny cars by my uncles, or followed my cousins on and off of buses whose numbers I never thought to notice, and now I stood across from the Termini station with my large backpack, with neither a map nor a guide, unsure which way to walk to get to my hostel.

At the time I thought it would be simple, I would find Vietri at his apartment, explain who I was, and ask him to tell me about the books. I had no other way to contact him, it had been four months since I'd left California, and his final order had come almost six months before I'd left the store. I'd set tasks like this for myself during my travels, on my arrival in various countries. Without an overarching purpose I'd had to give my wandering some form, I wasn't in search of a spiritual path or chasing surfing spots, and so I found I had to have my own small goals, like beads on a string. So I would search out the childhood homes of authors I admired, would visit the crypts of various patron saints, would witness the conjoining of great rivers, their waters separate in their own currents and colored sediments until they were no longer. At first I thought this would be similar, an afternoon, a conversation, Vietri amazed that someone from the store in California he had ordered all of those strange books from had found him, and was interested in his story.

As it happened, I did not arrive at 147 via Bevanda until my third day in Rome. I'd put it off, sleeping jet-lagged though the first afternoon, on my second wandering the garden paths of the Villa Borghese with a book and a bottle of water, alone, as I'd often wished I were in those previous summers. His apartment was in a quieter, more residential area, the bus ride that morning had taken me an hour from my hostel, and the buildings had fallen squat into a bland postwar architecture as we moved north. The apartments of this neighborhood were thin brick, with more variation than the yellows and salmons of the rest of the city, some were white, some Pepto-Bismol pink, and the balconies slotted on top of one another like crustless white bread sandwiches. As I walked from the bus stop, I noticed the faces around me all seemed to reflect a particular mix of anguish and awe, but in contrast I approached the metal panel of door buzzers outside the gate of 147 with a sense of lightness, the gold nameplates reflecting the sunlight, with black letters, Vietri's apartment number missing the plate and so exposing the steel hollow behind. My recent travels had given me the feeling that I moved on a different plane of existence than in California, with its friendly openness, the geographical foci of hills, ocean, mountains, instead, those months had been full of dislocations, so that I felt in a near constant state of reorienting which, rather than exhausting me, merely served to put me at a calm sense of remove from my own reality. It seemed to me that few things I'd done or would do could ever truly matter, and I'd come to enjoy this feeling, and take comfort in it, wondering how long I could float above the world until someone called me down with the answer of how to spend my years.

However, when pressing the buzzer in short bursts spaced a minute or so apart yielded nothing, I experienced an unexpected feeling of disappointment that verged quickly into sadness. I was surprised by my surprise, my naivete in believing Vietri would be easy to locate. It was possible Vietri was simply out of town, after all it was August and Rome was half empty, but I'd had a simple vision, of casually dropping by, of finding him home, of talking to him about his books, learning his story, of reclaiming a small bit of the Berkeley community of letters I'd abandoned, and I now watched this vision slip away from me, my useless fingers unable to grab it back.

I stepped away from the metal gate and turned south, back toward the river. I ignored the bus sign on its solitary pole, deciding to walk, first along the row of pines with their top-heavy, horizontal spreads, then the she-wolf rendered in concrete at the start of the bridge, her expression worried, or perhaps pained by her swollen teats and the strange children crouched beneath her, and the enormous fascist eagles perched along the pillars wore expressions of comical grumpiness, and I continued past all of it, still wanting. And it was in this way that I proceeded with my search for Vietri, pursuing a simple goal by direct methods yet drawn somewhere I could not have foreseen, the way that people lost in the woods drift inevitably to the side of their dominant hand, making enormous arcs that result, ultimately, in circles.

The next day another visit to the apartment yielded nothing, though I'd chosen a different time of day, the late afternoon. It was a Saturday, and Rome was blurrier, its movements more languid. I decided, walking away from the via Bevanda for the second time, that I should look for an obituary. The nameplate was missing, if the apartment was empty I might as well know if Vietri was still alive, and I felt frustrated, impatient, I was excited by the idea of a task for the afternoon. I'd thought of buzzing the other apartments in the building at random, asking if they knew this particular neighbor, but it had been so long since I'd spoken Italian, I cringed at the scenario in which I understood nothing, was not understood, or the one where my first question was, do you speak English? Besides, I was of the last generation that did not take for granted the joy of hiding behind a computer screen.

I went into the first internet café I passed on my way back to the hostel. I sat myself before a slightly outdated PC, trying to avoid eye contact with the teenage boy at the computer next to mine, fastidious in his search for photos of dark-skinned swimsuit models, occasionally copying choice images into a desktop folder. I'd never liked the Italian word for obituary,

necrologio, I had always found it aggressive, I suppose because it wore its association with death so plainly. I preferred
the couching of the English word, the vagueness of the vowel
sounds, its Latin root associated death with a downward
motion, a gentler worldview perhaps than the Greek word,
nekros, which carried as it moved itself through the Latin an
association with death by violent means. But in the *Corriere*,
entering a search for his surname, I found only the news of the
death of Martina Vietri, a nun in Illinois, in *La Repubblica*,
only an article about the migration of those under forty out of
Italy, quoting Alessandro Vietri, a Milanese sociologist. There
was no way to tell if they were relations, but I copied links to
both articles and saved them in a folder of email drafts. I didn't
know what good saving them would do, I was aware this was
an unusual project, but my curiosity was like a beast in my
chest, and besides, I had nothing else to fill my days.

Most of the Google results, when I searched for "Giordano
Vietri" for the first time since leaving the bookstore, remembering suddenly those long afternoons, were for a small coastal
town and a famous pottery company. I'd assumed the company was named for the town, but I tried the name of the company with the words employee list and founder, then business
profile, hoping I was choosing the right words in my clumsy
Italian, the letters strange through my fingers as I typed them.
The article I found was on the third or fourth page of results,
somewhere I'd never have looked if I'd had any plans in Rome,
any people I'd been eager to meet. The article profiled a new
manager of the company, overseeing a new factory opening,

and it featured a brief quote from a man who had been with the company at the beginning, a man named Giordano, with no last name given. It wasn't much, given the number of men in this country named Giordano, but I dragged it into the email draft with the rest of the links.

I stopped by Vietri's apartment building two more times over the next few days, though I'd mostly given up hope of finding him home. I hadn't originally planned to stay this long in Rome, knew I should reach out to my aunts and other relations, but I assumed they had abandoned the city for the August holiday, I thought I would wait until they returned to let them know I was in town and enact the brief reunion. I would press the buzzer a few times at evenly spaced intervals, then turn back to the street, heart racing, half expecting to be stopped and questioned. But on my fourth approach to the building I saw two teenage boys walking toward me down the plant-lined side of the building, part driveway, part alley, part courtyard. There was a gray gate for cars, another one, smaller, for pedestrians. The driveway led down into what must be parking spaces below, one entered the building before then with a sharp right into the lobby. They held the gate open for me politely and incuriously, and I slipped inside the building through the propped-open door. The pale orange staircase was quiet, and I climbed it slowly, rehearsing a few sentences in Italian even though I couldn't believe Vietri would be home, even though his letters had always been in English. As

I ascended I remembered the bookstore viscerally, its ladders and stepstools, the feeling of a stack of books against my torso as I leaned back to balance them, the way we assembled Vietri's books in their boxes before we shipped them to him, like trim size with like, slipping the boxes into enormous loose-weaved M-bags so that they would suddenly resemble parcels abandoned on a train platform in some earlier time, left by some other flood of refugees.

I knocked loudly on the apartment door, waited a few moments, and had raised my fist to knock a second time when the door to the adjacent apartment, just to my left, was flung open. A thin woman, wearing a green blouse that was both flamboyant and devastatingly severe, eyed me suspiciously. Surprised, all I could manage was "Cerco il signor Vietri." She gave a small negative movement to her head, and I continued in Italian, I came from California, is he home? Does he still live here? Her eyes narrowed, and she still hadn't spoken. Is he alive? I asked finally, my hands spreading before me. Something in her manner shifted, and it seemed she had made a decision. She leaned forward out of her doorway, and in Italian so rapid I felt sure it was intended to confuse me began a monologue that started as a list of things she could be doing that were better than talking to me about that silly old man, she continued, and I caught words as I could, but he's not here, he hasn't been here, not that he was much help when he was here, where had he been with all of their problems, they'd had no cooking gas for a week in June, didn't I see how the trash piled up, this city, as if it's not hard enough, didn't I know how hard it was to raise a child, and, listen, maybe her mother would have known it all, but she's dead now, isn't she?

I was feeling knocked askew by the force of her narration but summoned the courage to jump on the pause and ask, is there any way for me to contact him? In response to which question her Italian sped up even more and she began giving me directions to a café with pink germaniums outside, rosa, she emphasized, lurching forward suddenly, and told me to ask there, but how could she promise me anything because who knew about crazy old men and didn't she have enough problems? As the door swung closed I saw a toddler approaching with tyrannosaur-like unsteady bipedal steps, arms held out to his mother.

The café was only three or four storefronts down from the apartment gate, and this proximity made me think that the neighbor had intentionally complicated her directions. It had been the most forceful human interaction I'd had in weeks, and I felt off-kilter, strangely emotional as I walked toward the entrance. There were pink geraniums framing the door, in pots far too large for the small clumps of flowers. When I stepped inside the café the man behind the counter bellowed DI-ME in the way of all Roman cappuccino makers, but I waited until I had walked, at a measured pace, to the counter before explaining in a soft voice, my Italian suddenly shaky, that I was looking for il signor Vietri and I'd been told to come here.

The man, as he listened to this explanation, was constantly clearing his throat, then coughing in the deep-lung way of decades-long smokers into a white handkerchief with a delicate blue border. He'd bent down into his hand as another cough shook his torso, his large stomach pressed against the white buttons of his white shirt, but as his face angled down his eyes continued to meet mine so that it looked, his irises raised to the top edge of his lids, like a supplication. So it was that when he finally said something, the second half of it was swallowed into the most violent cough yet, and what I thought I'd heard him say was Chia—, before the word disappeared, and I thought that he'd wanted me to clarify, so I nodded and started to explain, staring as I did at the white tufts of hair exploding from his ears, but he immediately turned and went into the back room. When he came out he was holding a large, flat cardboard box in his hands, and as he handed it to me he said, his voice suddenly clear, pleasure to meet you at last, Chiara, and I realized then that he thought that my name was Chiara.

I opened my mouth to correct him, but then, my mouth moving toward the shape of an O and then closing, I found that I did not correct him. Instead, I tucked the box under my arm, thanked the man, assured him it had been a pleasure to have met him, and feeling or imagining all of the eyes of the café on my back, I turned and left the building.

Empty streets usually made me feel vulnerable while traveling, but that morning my mind was racing as I walked, barely aware of the blocks passing until I zeroed in on a bench near the river, running my fingers up and down the ridges in the cardboard, impatient to discover its contents. I breathed in deeply, trying to disperse the adrenaline flooding my system, I could practically feel it at the ends of my fingertips, straining to get out. I knew I could never go back to that café, could never try again to talk to that neighbor. My impulsive decision to go along with the mistaken identity—to steal whatever was in this box, though of course I didn't think of it as a theft at the time—still, I did know that whatever it was I had done would be irrevocable. I would not be returning shamefaced to confess as my father had once forced me to do at the age of three, when I'd grabbed a foil-wrapped piece of chocolate from the counter of the local drugstore, already melted and useless in my fist by the time we'd made the walk back across the parking lot through the Central Valley heat. Rather than reinforcing any sense of right and wrong in me, this episode, so deep in my early life I sometimes wondered if it had been a dream, made a different resolution harden, I determined that whatever I did, I would not be caught. The box would be all I had to go on.

I sat on the bench, weighing it in my hands. The box was heavy, dense and centered in the way that small animals are, made of cardboard flaps tucked expertly upon each other so that only one piece of tape held it closed. I slit open the tape with the key to my locker at the hostel, and as I slid my fingers inside I hesitated a moment, as if the contents could nip me. In my pinched fingers, out came a book.

It was made of cheap, thin paper, with a long dotted script

straining from its baseline in all directions. Inside were pages of maps, charts, lists, occasional illustrations of buildings, diagrams of wells. The maps showed squares arranged along what I assumed were roads, to one side wavy lines I thought indicated water. The calligraphy was beautiful and uniform, and only the smudges of the ink showed me it had been printed instead of handwritten. I found myself reading, though I understood nothing, my eyes traced the lines from right to left, as if I'd passed into a mirrored world. The bench on which I'd sat had no back, was just three roughly hewn pieces of stone, so I sat perpendicular and cross-legged with the book in my lap, my spine curved over it in a position that felt suddenly maternal, as a young couple passed by and I shielded it from view.

As I walked back toward the hostel that day I felt unmoored, by the Arabic I assumed I'd been reading, the Italian in the air around me. There was a sense of uncertainty that had arisen in my mind, was this the Tiber, were we now in the third millennium? Rome had always been a surreal city to me, the clocks all bearing different times, the cobblestones thick as grenades, so different from the smooth pavements of my childhood, the names of the streets camouflaged into one of eight angles on the sides of stone buildings, unlike the aggressively signed streets of Sacramento, the heat murky and strange compared to the dry oppression of the Central Valley. It was also true that all of my previous time in Rome had been spent being inducted into a new family system, so different from the quiet, tense triangle of my father, my mother, and me. It was all cousins, chaos, merging and fracturing alliances, my grandfather a passive patriarch, shuddering in my uncle's small cars through streets that were of a different genus entirely than the wide-laid suburban ones I'd grown up with. I remembered trying to describe to my cousins riding a bike to the community pool or the library, the way I'd spent my previous summers, the roads flat and calm, and knowing I'd failed.

For the first time I imagined my father arriving in Rome with his Italian wife on the one visit they'd made together before I was born. He would have researched the city and its dangers in his methodical way, would have prepared for razor blades to part open the bottoms of backpacks on the metro, for purses to be swiped by men on Vespas from the backs of outdoor café chairs, for the water to sit mosquito-heavy in the streets after the rains, though he was an admirer of Roman infrastructure, I'd heard him quote, on multiple occasions, the "What have the Romans done for us?" speech from *Monty Python's Life of Brian* to explain what civil engineers did. He had made himself ready for this, for evening sunburns, family interrogations, meals made up of the strange parts of cows, digestives that reminded him of mouthwash. But I don't believe that he was prepared to love the city, to love the family, as he would say simply and mournfully to me decades later, "I had a lovely time." Those two weeks made it worse, I knew, when his wife of this city, of this family, vanished from him, though it had always been clear to me that he'd kept this love for Rome, and for my mother, estranged from him, and from herself, as she was. He'd never come back to Rome, instead it was me, her daughter, who'd been sent back.

Chapter Three

I decided to email my cousin Andrea. It had been a decade since I'd last seen him, my father had first started sending me to Rome for the summers when my mother had gone away in middle school, saying it was important that I get to know this side of my family, though I'd always suspected he wouldn't have known what to do with me alone in the house over those long Californian school-less days. I stopped going once I was sixteen and could get a summer job, convincing my father it was more important for me to get work experience to put on my college applications, and once I left for college I'd stayed in Berkeley for the breaks instead of returning to Sacramento, finding cheap sublets and working my minimum-wage jobs at delis and libraries. I'd still talk to my aunts once a year, early on Christmas morning, the sounds of a large family on their side of the line, the quiet on mine. I'd answer their occasional emails with guilt, too briefly, and after too much time had passed, I never felt I had anything to report. My cousins had begun to befriend me on Facebook in the last year or two, and sometimes I looked through their photos, sometimes they commented on mine. But I knew it was a shallow way to have this family.

I recognized Andrea's tall frame as he approached my table at the café where we'd arranged to meet in San Lorenzo, near the bottom border of the Sapienza campus, his brown hair almost, but not quite, as light as mine. He still wore the worried expression I remembered from our teenage years, when his face had seemed to reflect some constant offstage tragedy, but it had softened somewhat, his eyes were darker and gentler than I remembered. It wasn't exactly that I was closest to Andrea, out of all of my family members, but we were only three months apart, had been thrown together from the beginning. It had surprised me that he had stayed in town for the holiday, wasn't off with the rest of the family, but perhaps this was our true kinship, he also had a desire for occasional solitude.

We met the day after the appeals court admitted the DNA evidence used to convict Amanda Knox had been unreliable, and her soft face angled up toward us from a newspaper abandoned on the next table. "You look like her, you know, bionda," Andrea said, after he'd kissed my cheeks and folded himself into his chair while lighting a cigarette. He'd called me that nickname the whole summer I'd turned fifteen, the last summer I'd spent in Rome, after we'd been separated at the Sunday market in Porto Portese and he'd found me shaken, on the verge of tears, because a man had been following me, calling me bionda, bionda. "But I'm not a blonde," I remembered saying, which Andrea had found hilarious. It was still true, I thought to myself. With my light brown hair, in America, I was not a blonde.

Andrea ordered us two espressos, dismissively, without asking what I wanted, and I found I was glad for this, I had never been able to keep track of the hours of the day in which it was

appropriate or horrific to instead drink a cappuccino. We settled into a conversation, he asked about my travels, and I tried
to figure out exactly what he was studying without asking directly. I knew he was still a student, but I could never remember the subject, maybe economics? I tried to parse clues, but
he mostly complained about his advisor, who he could never
find or get to answer emails but could not make any official
progress without, a conference he'd just been to in Athens.
On what? I asked hopefully. Cities, he said apathetically. On
his part, I could tell he was trying to figure out why I was in
Rome, how long I had been here, how long I would stay, prod-
ding at my casual explanations, I'd left my job, I'd been traveling, and why not? We spoke in English, the way we always had
when we were teenagers. I'd always assumed this was his way
of proving he hadn't suffered in education from being part of
the family that had stayed in Italy, no one else in the family
usually bothered, except my mother's older sister, Giulia, and
I was surprised to find that our conversation despite all of this
was not awkward, even if it was not warm. I realized I'd been
nervous only when I felt my leg muscles relax under the table,
somewhere away from my conscious brain, I'd half expected
him to be mad at me. The light reflected on the building behind us was just beginning to change when he lit another cigarette without breaking eye contact and exhaled. I told him I
wanted to ask a favor. What do you need? he replied in Italian, and I realized that his voice always sounded kinder in this
language. The one conversation I could remember having
with him in Italian, I thought as I looked back at him, as I

weighed my answer to what it was I needed, was when he'd asked me to tell him what had happened to my mother.

My Roman family, especially of the older generations, acknowledged no boundaries between themselves, and it had been hard for me, I'd grown up with so much solitude, the only child in a suburban house and preoccupied parents. Their word for privacy was the English word, il privacy, my relatives had no native concept of it in the abstract. But Andrea had the ironic distance of all Italians our age, I didn't need to worry about this turning into an emotional imploring of my duties to the family, and I had always felt that he understood, a little, more than anyone else, anyway. I needed help, and here he was before me.

I need to find someone who can read Arabic, I said, and he nodded.

Andrea had a friend who studied Arabic literature, they knew each other from a soccer club connected to the university, and this Giancarlo opened the door to his apartment in a worn Bob Marley t-shirt. He had a stooping posture that made him seem shorter than Andrea, though he was in fact taller, and seeing them next to each other had an unsettling effect as my eye traveled uncertainly between the tops of their heads, Giancarlo's curls looping and dark. Andrea was asking him about his holiday, he'd just gotten back into town, August was almost over, he had been with his family in Lecce. I followed them both into the apartment. Giancarlo moved quickly through the room while bantering with Andrea in a mess of words that was difficult for me to follow, and soon the book was out of my hands, had been placed among the collection of cigarette butts on the table. I wanted to tell him to be more careful with it, I had no idea what the book was, but it was unique in its possible connection to Vietri, as far as I knew there was no other book like it in the world, and even if it was mass-produced, even if there were a million of them, this one was mine and in the way of being twenty-five I didn't know if anything so precious would ever be given freely to me again. I imagined Vietri's hands on these pages and it was enough, this tactile feeling connecting us, the dark paper gray and smooth, slippery, the lines imprecise. But Giancarlo's energy was so transferable, he was eager to please, and so I ignored the small tendrils of imagined catastrophes creeping along the backboards of my mind, the lit cigarette in the tray, the white ceramic cups of espresso uncertainly balanced, and let myself become absorbed in his monologue. We sat together at the large table, and the book spread open before us covered almost a third of it. It was from Palestine, he said, a village history. Al-Tantura, he read, running his fingers along the title as if reading braille. He kept up a rapid stream of words in Italian, while I tried to translate into English in my head. All that remains, I caught. Andrea was leaning back in his chair, eyes on his cell phone, and Giancarlo maintained a loud murmur only half of which I understood. He turned the pages rapidly, decisively, reading out loud, while every so often I would reach out to stroke a margin, to reassure myself that it was still there, was still mine.

Did the book describe a village? I asked, and he shook his head in something like frustration, though Giancarlo was so jovial it hardly came out as a negative emotion. Andrea got up and began busying himself in the kitchen with Giancarlo's other roommates, only half-glimpsed forms to me through the open door, making the sounds boys make when they are speaking unseriously among themselves. He said he'd been reading me the names, the professions, the surnames that labeled the structures on the maps, but, I interrupted, what's it about? Giancarlo gave me a perplexed look, and said that if I really wanted to meet with someone who could explain it, he had a colleague—I noted the *a* that terminated that word, a female colleague then—an anthropologist, he clarified, who studied this sort of thing. We were looking at the pieces, he continued, and she would know the whole. Can we meet her? I asked. Andrea had come back into the room then, or rather he stood in the doorway, and I saw him exchange a look I could not read with Giancarlo, who then checked the time on his cell phone and stood up, motioning for me to follow him and mumbling something I couldn't understand while he slipped on a jacket, despite the August heat. I hadn't meant to suggest meeting his friend the anthropologist at that immediate moment, didn't these people have anything else to do? But, as I'd learned from Andrea during our chat at the café, dottoratos, which they all were, basically PhD students, neither taught nor took classes, they had no jobs or internships, and the economy being what it was, they all tried to pursue these educations for as long as possible, so no, they didn't have anything else to do, and anyway, the words to correct what I'd meant didn't arrive in Italian. A thrill moved through me as I followed Giancarlo out the door, as Andrea turned his attention from Giancarlo's roommates and waved goodbye to me from across the room dismissively, or warily.

Outside the apartment building, Giancarlo unlocked a scooter and handed me the helmet, and I put it on but didn't tighten the straps. Once he sat down, I climbed on behind him, tentatively holding his sides, and we pulled off his crooked street onto the via Tiburtina. The traffic was heavy, but the movements had an underlying grammar, a flow, that made sense to me, and I leaned into Giancarlo on the turns, idly imagined moving my palms to press against his stomach. It had been some time since I'd been this close to another person. It began to rain, lightly, the drops surprisingly cold on my bare arms. South Asian umbrella vendors were appearing on the sidewalk next to us as we waited at a light, withdrawing cheap black umbrellas from huge duffel bags like swords and shouting "cinque euro" as they waved them flamboyantly. I worried about the book in my cheap cloth bag, currently lodged between Giancarlo's back and my stomach, and I thought about asking into his ear if we should stop, but the light changed and we drove on, his gaze fixed on the road ahead, and it was a relief, after traveling by myself for so long, to surrender decision making entirely. We drove for another twenty minutes, away from the city's center, to a neighborhood full of tall apartment blocks, all two-toned uniform rectangles flanked by wide dusty expanses colored gray in the rain. Giancarlo parked the scooter outside one of these buildings, locked it carefully to itself, and only then turned to me solicitously, asking if I'd gotten too wet, and jogging with me to the doorway of the building, his arm guiding me at the center of my back. I had no idea what neighborhood we were in, certainly we were on the outskirts of the city, but Giancarlo moved confidently through the street. There was more garbage strewn on the road here, and in the apartment building where Giancarlo led me the staircase was dark. An open door at one landing let me glance, quickly, into an apartment where a dozen people of more than two generations were in various poses of rest and play across the floor. I followed Giancarlo farther up the dark stair, and heard him call ahead of me, through the thin door, Laura, eccomi.

Laura opened her door, and I could see her surprise at seeing me behind Giancarlo. I'd taken the book out of my bag and had held it to my chest as I climbed, trying to assess any damage, brushing away imagined drops of water, hoping they would absorb into my shirt, the skin of my palms. Giancarlo stooped down to kiss Laura's cheeks, she was short, shorter than I was, her dark head like a small animal pulling away, and I heard her muttering disapprovingly, maybe pleading, I couldn't make out any of the words. He pulled her partway into the apartment so that I could no longer see their faces, and after a few awkward seconds curled the top half of his body around the open door and beckoned me inside.

Giancarlo had told me that Laura was an anthropology

student who did a lot of work in Lebanon and Syria, and once inside the large and dark apartment he made a joke about her slow progress toward her degree, punctuating this sentence by pinching my arm playfully. His large hand fit over my entire biceps, as if squeezing a tube to see if it was hollow, and I wondered if he was trying to flirt with me, if it was to make Laura jealous, and I felt weary. Laura glanced at the neckline of my shirt and offered me a coffee. Giancarlo followed Laura into the small kitchen, asking something about her roommates, leaving me in the main room, and I thought about how I hadn't had a conversation alone with another woman in a long time. While traveling I'd gravitated toward men in small groups, joining them for a city or two before detaching to go my own way. I found traveling with guys to be easier, I was less likely to be hassled and I felt safer, but also the leaving was easier, there were no promises to email extracted, often it was just a hand gesture at a bus station as we boarded separate vessels.

I'd remained standing in the living room, and through the sliver of the open kitchen door I could see Giancarlo moving comfortably around Laura, who leaned back against the counter with her arms folded, he was taking cups down carefully from the wood cabinets as if he were handling small pieces of her soul, moving his lips gently, her head shaking occasionally in response. They came out and Laura set down a large bottle of water and glasses on the coffee table and I pretended to have been looking at the bookshelves. I perched myself uncomfortably on a plastic chair, and they sat opposite me on the sofa. Laura's face was sharp, angular, her small dark eyes had the unstill, jumpy quality of a rodent's, yet she spoke slowly and clearly. "The thing you need to understand," she said in English, though Giancarlo had been speaking to me in Italian, "is that this trauma moves through generations." She drew out the vowels on the word trauma so that each one encompassed its own syllable, making it rhyme with the Italian pronunciation of her own name. She described the decades-ago war that led to the destruction of these villages—not destruction, erasure, complete erasure, she said, and she continued without a pause, telling me of the refugee camps that she had visited, where the people from these villages had gone afterward; about the policy of the Italian Red Cross to send its members to these camps no more than three times; how some of the members, over the course of these three visits, had seen entire generations grow up: the babies they first met have their own children, then grandchildren, still in the camps, waiting. Laura ran her finger around the top of her cup, now empty.

As we walked down the stairs of the apartment building, I realized that I had been so caught up in Laura's monologue it hadn't occurred to me that we hadn't even discussed the book. I said as much to Giancarlo as we approached his scooter, the day sunny again, the water evaporating as thick steam from the pavement. He shrugged. "Yes, we will have to go back."

I had asked Andrea, when I'd first emailed him, not to tell the rest of my family I was in Rome. September was approaching, I knew they'd be back soon, the population of the city would switch out after the end of the August flight, but I wasn't ready, not yet, for the full reunion. The web of my family in Rome extended into the dozens, and starting with Andrea felt achievable to me, the way when making certain cakes one must introduce only a small portion of the melted chocolate into the egg mixture so as not to produce a scramble. We'd met for a drink in San Lorenzo, were sitting outside in comfortable heat, one drink that neither the waiter nor Andrea ever moved to replenish. I'd waited for Andrea for half an hour past the time we'd agreed to meet, and when I'd complained, he'd mimicked the annoyed gesture I'd made and asked when I would get a cell phone. I'd answered that I wasn't staying in Rome. In the week since I'd last seen him, since the day I'd met Giancarlo and Laura, none of them had emailed me, and I'd felt shy about contacting them.

I hadn't planned to spend more than a few days in Rome, but I was beginning to see how time could move differently here. I'd been afraid of long empty hours that actually passed quickly by me. I had had a job since I was sixteen, these last months of travel were my first time since then not working, and I found myself on a slippery expansion into a life without constraints on my time, the borders of myself no longer had any boundaries to push against and I felt seduced by the nihilism of such a life, comforted by its hopelessness. My sightseeing in Rome had been confined to that first blurry summer when I was eleven, passed every day to a different aunt or cousin who plainly resented the embarrassing fact of their presence at the Vatican or the Colosseum. After the first two weeks it was assumed I'd been shown everything the family had decided I should see, and I faded into the background with the rest of my generation. Now, though, the water from a fountain in a half-crumbled stone wall catching the light, I felt a vague curiosity stir.

I spent most of my time that week wandering the streets, often thinking of Vietri, speculating about the strange book and his connection to it. I especially liked walking along the river, drawn to the enormous sycamores that grew there. In California their branches were trimmed down year after year to keep them from growing into the electrical wires above, so that the original branches would spread and clump as the offshoots were removed, and they'd always, in this deformed state, reminded me of an upraised fist whose fingers had been amputated at the first knuckle. Here they grew to their true height, their crowns broad and full, appearing only slightly related to their stunted cousins.

I had so few memories of the time I'd spent in Rome as a teenager, those four, or was it five? summers seemed to be one long unbroken stretch of time in which I watched television with my cousins, trashy reality competitions or long specials on RAI of elderly musicians I'd never heard of, locked myself in the bathroom for hours trying to teach myself to shave my legs, emerging only once I'd been able to stop the bleeding from the deep nicks on my ankles and knees, helping my aunts cut up vegetables, chided for being so quiet while with the same breath they continued their overlapping monologues, reading, mostly, in whatever room I could find empty in whatever apartment I'd found myself in. There'd been several apartments we moved between, were often at one of my aunts', but I mostly remembered my grandparents', with its dark tall walls and wood paneling, its tiles and its odors, the silhouette of my grandfather in the corner.

I'd never met my grandmother, but she was a presence in the house, as alive to my aunts as I was, she moved in the air between us. She'd died when I was two, when my mother was having her "problems," before things had been "calm" enough to bring me over to meet her. My grandmother's cancer had taken up the last months of her life, and my aunts were frank in their belief that my parents had had plenty of time to do so, and I was her only granddaughter. My cousin Claudia, really my grandmother's niece, had been named after her, but we called her Dida, her sister's toddler invention. I'd been given my grandfather's name, though in America Gabriele was clearly the name of a girl.

Dida was the one who'd showed me how to shave my legs, finally, she'd caught me exiting the bathroom with a wad of toilet paper on my shin for a particularly deep cut, parallel to the bone. She was the most aloof of my cousins, she and Clea, her sister, were a few years older, and while Clea followed me around asking me questions about California, knew more about the people on MTV than I did, tried to sit as close to me on the couch as possible as if she could absorb a foreign essence, Dida was the one who brought me to the pharmacy and showed me which razors to buy. I'd been shaving with the single-bladed boys' Bics my father bought me, left with no announcement at the entrance to my bedroom in a Rite Aid bag along with boxy menstrual pads. It would take me until college to learn how to effectively use a tampon.

At that moment in time the thought of seeing the rest of my cousins exhausted me. The closest I came to understanding this reluctance was a memory I had of the time they'd all realized at the same moment I did that I didn't know how to open the door to my grandparents' apartment from the inside. Instead of a doorknob there was a metal box and two bars running up and down the length of the door, with a keyhole next to a protruding metal half circle that I tried in vain to rotate, then push. I'd finally looked back at the group of them watching, and asked uncertainly if I needed the key. They'd all laughed, and it was true, it was almost the end of the summer and it was ridiculous that I didn't know how to open the door, but I'd never been first in line out of the apartment, had never left it on my own. Andrea was the one who had stepped forward and slid the metal circle to the side, opening the door.

Andrea's mother, my mother's younger sister, was named Settimia, after an aunt who had been the seventh daughter, the father had run out of names. But now the generations were tapering down, the Italians, I had always thought cynically, having finally connected the increase in lifestyle quality with the decrease in mouths to feed, so it was in my family, Andrea and I were both only children. Italy's birth rate was now 1.2, far from replicating, the city had expanded and contracted, again sucking the world into its borders, the children I saw now in Rome were in no small part the children of parents from elsewhere. But out of these top-heavy older generations, Settimia was the only one who, I felt, didn't blame me for what had happened, because it was while pregnant, in a new country, at the age of twenty-five, that my mother, as they referred to it, "changed." I had never heard anyone in the family there use the word schizophrenic.

Chapter Four

When Giancarlo finally emailed me he addressed me as if we'd parted moments before and suggested I come with him to Laura's apartment that Thursday, after they were done with their university obligations. I wondered what to do in the meantime, it was only Sunday. I thought about the book, safe in my hostel locker. Whatever was written there, I decided, it was probably not a direct course to Vietri, it was no treasure map or diary. Maybe he was the author, maybe he had a relationship to its subject, but it seemed unlikely based on his book orders, they'd never had a particular geographic focus on the Middle East. Whatever his connection to Palestine, I thought I might as well pursue other paths in the meantime.

Since I'd failed to find an obituary, I decided to proceed on the assumption that Vietri was still alive. I spent several afternoons scanning the online staff directories of universities, archives, libraries, calling the ones that had none listed on their websites, giving Vietri's name, but without luck. The next day I visited the handful of academic bookstores in Rome, annoying the clerks by asking if they had any peculiar customers who read a lot, or strangely, but unsurprisingly these interrogations got me nowhere, except to remind me how blunt Romans could be to strangers they considered dull, but they were useful nevertheless, after these efforts it became clear to me that

Vietri was no academic, that I would never find him through association with the books that had so fascinated me.

At that point, I thought perhaps what I should do next was to try to look up a birth certificate. I'm not sure what I thought a birth certificate might tell me, but at least, I imagined, it would tether my search to the real world, would be something tangible for me amidst all of my thoughts and conjectures, would prove that my search could have a conclusion, could have, or had had at one point, a body. I obtained the request form online, I'd had to track down a few documents like this to claim my citizenship, and perhaps it was nothing more than my mind, my fingers, following paths they already knew. I had to submit it to the commune of birth, basically the township, as well as the province, and I chose Rome, listed Vietri's address, left his date of birth and the names of his parents blank. At the line requesting my name and information, I hesitated, I thought I remembered that personal records might only be available to family members, but I wasn't sure, I couldn't remember, the form gave no indication. After a few minutes of staring down at the piece of paper I'd paid two euro to print, I wrote Chiara Vietri and the address of the hostel. I put it in the mail slot quickly, addressed to the Ufficio dello Stato Civile.

The hostel I'd found was near the Piazza Bologna, neither central nor cheap enough to be a true party hostel, but still, it was Rome, it was August, and in the mornings there was the sticky-sweet smell of spilled limoncello in the air, occasional vomit outside on the curb, wet bras and phone chargers draped along the top bunks, and I looked around sometimes and wondered what it was, this life that I thought I was living. I was frequently mistaken for much younger than I was, a fact that I was grateful for in these situations, especially as I crept toward the end of my twenties with nothing to show for my years. When people commented on this, I usually replied that I would probably follow the model of Italian women, looking eighteen until I was thirty-five when suddenly I would gain fifty pounds and sprout chin hairs. This hadn't happened to my mother, however, she had always been thin and painfully small, but I had always had great success with this joke and was reluctant to abandon it, though it was so far unproven by my own genes.

Neither of my parents was particularly funny, they were both engineers and serious, cautious in their spoken words, but I'd grown up an only child desperate to draw adults' attention. I developed a sarcastic and world-weary wit that I drew on like a shift, getting me through the prolonged social navigation of middle school and high school, though the probing questions of friends' parents that came when your own mother was mysteriously absent in what was, despite being the capital of the most populous state of one of the world's largest countries, a small, provincial, farmy town, and though I felt I could count on it I equally felt that it wasn't a true part of my nature. Sometimes in the last year, in between these big cities with their aggressively social hostel scenes, in the quieter weeks I'd spent by myself, I felt this trait, this self-effacing sociability, was wasted, and I wondered if it would still be there when I returned to claim it, and if not, what would be left.

Some nights I'd go to the hostel's basement bar with a book for a euro beer and a two-euro plate of pasta, and this was the way that I met Maria. She had stood uncertainly near the bar, holding her drink and surveying the crowded room. It was clear we were both alone, moreover that she was also older than our fellow travelers by a crucial few years, and it was those few years that led me to ask if she'd like to share my small table. Around us were Australians, Americans, Dutchmen, speaking loudly and bringing their drinks to their mouths with exaggerated gestures as if on a stage, the Americans the youngest, the Australians the most intent on drunkenness. There was an energy in the room I knew well from these hostels, it had to do with the possibility of sex, not of one couple's chemistry but that of many individuals, the kind of near infinite possibilities of coupling that I imagined gave rise to the universe and its subsequent forms of life. I said something to this effect to Maria, and she smiled in a downward direction and replied that she didn't know, she'd just gotten married when she started to travel. She and her husband had met in college, she told me, worked jobs they liked well enough for a few years after graduating, had saved, gotten married, then quit their jobs and planned to spend a yearlong honeymoon seeing the world before returning home and starting a family.

I'd met a few couples traveling together on these extended trips in South America, but they were rare. I imagined they stayed in hotels for the privacy, or weren't on these monthslong trips so common to the rest of us to begin with, that they had more settled lives, ones they couldn't depart. Moreover, I couldn't have imagined my months of travel without the freedom of being untied to a partner, the thrill of flirting, of sex, it had become a part of the changefulness inherent in my weeks, a different country, a different language, a different boy. It wasn't that the sex was always good, or that it was every night, or even every week, but I became addicted to the way these boys said my name while they were inside of me. I'd spent most of college with one boyfriend or another, and I'd loved not feeling any allegiance, not having my thoughts occupied, being able to say goodbye and wish them well and not worry about running into them again. I felt an overwhelming amount of tenderness toward the boys I'd slept with, all of them, even the ones who were too drunk to come or who told me, the next morning, about their girlfriends back home, afraid I would comment on their Facebook pages. These boys never asked why I was quiet, we took each other as we were in a way that was liberating, they were all nice guys, I stayed away from the creepers, the assholes, the really wild ones, I'd prided myself on having a sense for it, and so I would kiss very few boys I didn't sleep with as well. It had been helpful to me to stand next to these different boys and evaluate their reflection on my own self, which I was trying so hard to define, or leave behind, I wasn't sure which. And so I felt an over-rushing sense of tenderness toward all of them until suddenly I didn't, suddenly the fact that they were all the same, no matter what their nationalities were, no matter the things we did while together, no matter if it was a hostel bed or one of the love hotels in Argentina, suddenly this fact, that these boys were all the same, became heavy, and I'd felt as if I'd been skimming on a wave for years without noticing, and only now that I was underwater did I realize the weight I'd been acquiring the whole time.

I asked Maria to tell me about her travels with her husband, wondering idly where he was, appreciating how content she was with the silence between us. They'd gotten married just before they left, she said after a pause, and had chosen Bali as their first stop, had planned to stay there for a month, wanting to ease into traveling and not rush around immediately. They'd found a place through a network of worldwide organic farms where they could stay in exchange for work, where they imagined they would fall asleep every night tanned and exhausted, other travelers for company in the evenings, but with a private room, enough to enjoy the honeymoon.

When they arrived they found not so much a farm as a decrepit concrete house with a sickly looking vegetable garden. The Dutch woman who ran it came out to greet them before they reached the gate, surrounded by six or seven dogs, all bearing uncertain amounts of fur, barking fiercely as they approached, and the woman chastised Maria and her husband for appearing afraid, implying that if one of the dogs lunged it would be their fault.

Things did not improve. It turned out there was very little farmwork to do, the fields had been left fallow for a decade at least, and the Dutch woman really wanted their help to build a website and write it in English. She seemed to have, Maria said, a delusional idea that the property could become sort of a hotel or campground she could rent to tourists. To this end their room was not a room but a cheap tent pitched outside on hard dirt.

They stuck it out for a few days, hoping their impressions were wrong, that things would get better. They had some good times in the tent, she said, laughing about how mistaken they'd been about what it would be like. Then, Maria said, on the fourth morning her husband woke early and stepped outside the tent to pee. A dog neither of them had seen before, that her husband barely saw before it was on him, lunged for his leg, leaving behind a mess of blood, several barely attached pieces of skin and flesh, a small white bubble of saliva.

His scream woke her up, she said, and she grabbed a towel. It took almost an hour to stop the bleeding, she said, and it was the only thing she could think of. It was only later she thought of rabies. She looked for the dog for days, returning to the farm on a bicycle from the hotel they had booked in the nearest town for far too much money. She assumed they would go to Denpasar and get him the rabies vaccine as soon as possible, but he'd refused. The bleeding had stopped, and she'd cleaned the wound as best she could, now a huge bruise with three precise puncture marks. She spent her nights in the internet café, researching the disease, growing increasingly panicked, bringing him dinner and pleading with him. He refused to leave the hotel even when there was a taxi downstairs, and she, sobbing, gave it the fare for the trip back to the capital. Was this an early symptom, and it was already too late? Or was it something that had always been in him, but she'd never had the opportunity to notice? They'd been together for five years before they got married, and she couldn't remember him going to a doctor, but why would he? He was in his early twenties and in perfect health.

I started having panic attacks while bicycling to the farm, she continued. Once I even fell over, though usually I could stop in time by the side of the road. Oddly I was never scared for myself, even though I was intentionally out in search of what I believed to be a rabid dog, rather my panic was immense, universe-sized, encompassing everything I'd ever learned or experienced or believed to be true in the world. The first time I thought I was dying, it was like a heart attack, and I remember that part of me was glad, that in some way we would be dying together as we'd once discussed when very drunk. I never got used to them, each one was world-ending, when they were over it felt each time like I had to remake the earth around me, but I did develop a response, putting my head between my knees and ignoring everything, even passersby on the road who stopped to help. Once, my head down, I felt a hand on the underside of my skull, where you might hold an infant's. The attack was subsiding, and I was only beginning to be aware of sensations again, so I was unsure how long the hand had been there. Through my hair, I couldn't feel any skin contact, and I never raised my head, even after my breathing returned to normal. That hand held my head for what seemed like hours, and after it was gone, so gently removed I was never sure the moment it had left, after it was gone I waited much longer to finally move and cycle back to the hotel.

After two weeks my husband got the flu. Only once he was bedridden could I get a doctor in, earlier, in his delirium, he'd pushed the old man to the ground. Now he was too weak. It was awful. It was so hot, and he'd scream when we tried to get him to drink water. That's what they used to call rabies, you know, hydrophobia. The one thing you need is the thing you become most afraid of.

Did he die? I asked.

I had a hard time with bottled water after that, she continued. Not drinking the tap water in those countries, it forces you to plan, to be so aware of where your next sip is coming from. I had a really hard time with that. But I couldn't go home. I still had all the money we'd saved, in a joint account. We'd planned everything, I couldn't think of anything else to do but stick to the plan, and I have. Vietnam, Laos, Thailand, India, South Africa, now Europe. I took a boat cruise down the Mekong, I rode my bike through the Belgian breweries, spent a week on the beach in Croatia, everything we talked of doing, I showed up for everything we prebooked. And now Rome. It was supposed to be our last stop, a luxury before we went home, to have one more month on honeymoon. But what do I do now? The money is gone, my husband is gone, I don't know anything anymore. I've never seen more of the planet and I've never felt so unconnected to this earth, it's like my feet could lift up at any moment. I can't go back to Denver, our storage unit, his family. I don't know what to do now. I don't know where to go.

Maria was staring at a crack in the wall beside us, her eyes running up and down it as if she could see through it to the earth that surrounded us. Rome is so old, she said, I like it here. I like the layers. They say it grows an inch every ten years. And then all of a sudden they renovate a pizzeria and find some vault or millennia-old bedroom, and it was like it was never there before. But it's just accumulation. I think about the things that are lost every generation. This city has known so much and forgotten so much more. My husband was an architect. He loved this city. I never really listened when he would talk about it since I knew he would tell me again once we came here. And now I've been to so many countries it feels like my own has been erased. So, no home, no country, no job, no husband, just Rome. And what can I do with Rome? I should have tried harder to get a doctor. I should have hired strong men to force him into a taxi, to hold him down while we gave him the vaccine. I shouldn't have left him there. The worst is not knowing if it was him or the virus. They say it takes two weeks to affect the brain, but that means my husband was himself for the two weeks that could have kept him with me. I would kiss him while he lay in that hotel bed, I'd read it was possible to transmit mouth to mouth, I would kiss him deeply whenever he'd let me. It felt like the hotel was the whole world and if I left the world I would die.

I'd been studying Maria while she told her story, emboldened by the fact that she'd rarely looked at me, instead she'd spoken almost entirely in profile, her face sideways and now tilted up toward one of the narrow windows at the top of the basement bar, so that her posture resembled nothing so much as the beatific, saintly virgins rendered in pop blues and reds in Renaissance churches, their hair thin and pale against the splendor of the other colors. Maria's face was narrow, in contrast to those Madonnas, and angular without being sharp, and as I was thinking about these women and what they'd witnessed, my lips must have parted without me noticing. As if to cut off the question I hadn't yet repeated, Maria looked at me directly for the first time in several minutes.

I don't know, she said. If he is alive. After I got him to the hospital in Denpasar, I called his parents, then went straight to the airport and got on a flight to Bangkok. I didn't wait for them to arrive. They will probably never speak to me again. But they didn't understand, he was the one who had betrayed me. He was the one who left.

After a few minutes of silence, Maria stood up and left the bar, a good-night trailing behind her. I didn't follow her, or try to delay her with polite words, acquainted as I was with the sudden need for solitude after disclosing information of this type to strangers. People had always been inclined to tell me things, my features were my father's, wide-set and Germanic, my face naturally assumed a neutral, detached expression that encouraged the confessional, and this wasn't the first time during my travels that I'd been told a story the person needed to pour out of them into someone else. But my whole system felt knocked askew, I fiddled with my empty glass, tilting it to one side and letting it fall back to the table, this was the problem with deep empathy, it required action. I got up to refill my beer at the bar. Maria was trying to outrun her guilt, the loss of her husband, but what else was she to do?

The great uncertainty that hung over my life, the thing that prevented me from feeling that my life was real, that it belonged to me, was the dull and predictable fear of becoming like my mother. The average age for a female schizophrenia diagnosis was twenty-five, the same birthday I'd had a few months before coming to Rome, and the statistics varied, but as the daughter of a schizophrenic the chance my mind, my life, could disappear from me at any moment was around 10 percent. As my dad would have put it, great odds in Vegas. There was no test, no way to prediagnose, one was a schizophrenic when one manifested the symptoms of schizophrenia. This was why I never felt attached to that life with my boyfriend and the bookstore, why the increasing professional accomplishments of my peers had never truly bothered me. Why build a career, why build a life when I knew it could all disappear? I was waiting through this decade for the ground to remove itself from beneath me, to become a stranger to myself, so I estranged myself from my own life. As long as this was held over me, this swerve my life could take, I felt as if there were no point in striving for something, as my mother had. I was content to wait out my twenties, to do everything I could to not get pregnant, condoms and birth control, a liberal use of the morning-after pill when in doubt. This search for Vietri was another way to pass the time. Of course it occurred to me, of course I worried, that my interest in Vietri could be a sign of the type of obsessive and detached-from-reality thinking that could result in a diagnosis, but I had spent years being suspicious of my own mind, and it was it was like a scab I picked at, hoping for an infection to spread that wouldn't strictly be my own fault. I was traveling even though my mother's schizophrenia had been triggered in a foreign country, I knew on some level I was tempting it, but I also knew that if something was to happen I wanted it to happen, wanted to have my fate decided and move on. These months of travel had rocked me into a lull of complacency, I really thought that maybe they could continue forever, or at least until I was past the age where symptoms could appear. If they did, I knew I would give myself over to the disease, and if they didn't, then I would stand as if the sole survivor of a plague, surveying the ruined landscape. If something wasn't perfect I'd always had the impulse to destroy it, a way of being in the world I was just beginning to see as childish.

Chapter Five

Giancarlo picked me up outside the hostel late in the afternoon that Thursday and drove us to Laura's apartment. I'd felt uneasy with the demand on their time, but Laura, perhaps sensing my discomfort, had mentioned being able to cite the translation work for her graduate studies, and whether or not it was true, it was kind. I was interested in the village book, eager to see its mysteries unfold from the unknown script, drawn, too, to Giancarlo and Laura and the entanglement that I sensed awaited me there.

Our meeting that day was like a bizarre reading group, Laura and Giancarlo sitting next to each other, both bent over the book, Laura pushing up her glasses, Giancarlo making the same attempt at his hair, arguing about the meaning of this word or that, or if it was indeed this word or that, if this dot or that small brush of line changed the interpretation completely. Her fingers were long and thin, interrupted by bulbous knuckles, there was something grotesque about her thick unpolished nails that ran along the pages, their vertical ridges prominent, the tips yellowing. The book stayed on her lap while Giancarlo oriented himself around it. I sat across from them, smiling along as if I understood, translating what they said into my notebook, sometimes doodling, feeling childlike and oddly content.

I often couldn't understand what Giancarlo and Laura were saying, not only because their Italian was so rapid and complex, more and more, I realized, my family, even my mother, must have been speaking to me in circumscribed Italian, but also because they spoke with the peculiar slang and rhythms of serious couples, their words expanding backward and forward through time, pulling in their deep knowledge of each other sideways, so that following the trajectory of their sentences was especially hard to accomplish. My Italian had always been shaky, my first four or five years of life, when my multiplying brain synapses would have made the absorption of a second language fluid and easy, were "bad years" for my mother, and she'd lived with us infrequently. My parents had planned to raise me bilingual, but what could they do, my father didn't speak Italian. When my mother came home, during the "good years," the years before she went away again when I was eleven, it was already too late, I was in kindergarten, and she quickly became frustrated and spoke to me in English when I couldn't respond. When my mother spoke to me in Italian for those few short years, it was orders, it was questions, it was demands, and she never tried very hard, we never talked about the period of my life when she was gone, but she must have felt that with this gap, without this language, I would never be exactly like her, raised in her image, able to speak with the same continuation a whole life of Italian. I knew words and phrases, and I had the pronunciation, but it wasn't until I studied French in high school that the grammar fell into place. Then listening to my aunts and cousins on my visits became easier, but it was a shallow way to understand the language, as if words and tenses had been mapped onto the deep French grooves that I'd spent so much time studying. I loved learning French, when I spoke French it was Baudelaire and Aimé Césaire, it was debating politics in church basements for three-hundred-dollar prize checks, it was memorizing whole poems while passing time in class, "Mon enfant, ma soeur," it was getting the references in T. S. Eliot poems, it was being able to pronounce certain words in Chaucer when made to read aloud in Middle English. Italian was my cousins shouting at one another, making jokes I could barely begin to understand, some animal or another, jokes I could only hope weren't at my expense. I didn't know anyone who was French, I'd never been to France, it was the language of a contained reality, a perfect one I would never enter. Once in high school a friend asked if I wished our school had taught Italian instead, like some of the richer private schools in the Bay Area with their fourth generations of Luccesan pastry makers and bankers, and I'd responded that if the Italians had wanted more people to speak their language they should have been better at colonizing.

Giancarlo and Laura were continuing between their three languages, "Youadi," they said, over and over. Then, "Chia-mare." Some whispers about churches, Giancarlo making a gesture, as if from a pulpit, that owed more to the American South than to the Catholic services here. Then, finally, they turned to me, pleased. "It is a call and response," Laura said in English. Switching to Italian, she translated from the Arabic:

*We have put before you the names of the village lands,
part by part, the names of the springs and valleys, the
names of the pools and wells, the names of the fruit and
other trees, the names of the seasonal crops, and we give
you the responsibility, this charge, to you, the children and
grandchildren, who are the trustees...*

"It's answered by the grandchildren," Giancarlo explained,
but he didn't read their responses aloud.

I still didn't quite understand what it was we were translating, Giancarlo's explanation being, it's what they do to remember. I asked Laura the next time we were alone, when Giancarlo had gone out to buy cigarettes. He tended to talk over her enthusiastically, though I preferred her measured and direct explanations. Laura was suspicious of me, that was easy to see, her longing for Giancarlo was plain. But there was an earnestness in her, a desire to share this knowledge that her life had so far been devoted to that I could see overcoming her reluctance. I started in Italian, though I regretted it, Laura's English was much better, so that my clumsy question came out, what is the purpose of these books? Laura looked serious, then answered, they try to describe everything about the villages that are no longer there. Al-Tantura, it's a village that was destroyed in the war there, over fifty years ago. In general, she said, they were written by the elders of the villages, the old men, but written for the next generations, so that they could know that these villages had existed, that they had had homes, histories. That's why there are so many maps. You know, she said, her fingers

playing delicately over the top edge of the book, these are people who know they are going to die without seeing their homes
again because the homes no longer exist. Giancarlo and I, we
left our towns because they were so small, we had to, there are
no jobs there, but of course it is very hard in Rome with no
connections, we are near the end of our studies, we know there
are no jobs for us here. So we are stuck, neither of us can go
back to live in our towns again, now it's only the very old there,
we wouldn't be able to find work. But they still exist, at least
we can go back. I tried to remember where she'd said she was
from, and remembered only that she'd followed its name immediately with the fact that it was near Lecce, the way you do
when you know someone hasn't heard of the place. I'd often
done the same thing myself, when pressed to be more specific
than California, I'd learned to treat Sacramento qui vicino a
San Francisco as the Italian name for my hometown. Some of
them have been in the refugee camps for generations, Laura
continued. They do it to remind themselves, to remind their
children, that there was a world in which they also had landscapes and histories, where they were considered fellow people. She looked at me frankly. You understand.

Giancarlo came back into the room then and approached
each of us in turn, offering to make more coffee, a snack, a cigarette, it was so easy to see that he wanted everyone to be happy.
Laura was different, I saw now, and I turned this knowledge
over in my mind. I'd observed, in the academics who fre-
quented the bookstore, that whatever underlying impulse had
driven them to a particular subject, after only a few years

they were so deep under the water it was as if they'd always had these obsessions, this particular marine environment. I admired her self-awareness, the thought she'd given to the impulses underlying her own life. With Giancarlo, though it must have taken him years of intense study to become as fluent as he was, I could imagine the original impulse being based on nothing more than a passing thought. But then, of course, he'd devoted himself to it. I wondered what had brought him and Laura apart. It was clear they'd once been as intimate as any couple I'd seen, I could tell even from the way they oriented their bodies toward each other in a room, as if they each felt the gravitational pull of the other's circle. Giancarlo's motives were confused, I saw now, he was like a toddler who hadn't realized that the two things he wanted could not simultaneously exist, to use me to get to Laura but also to have me, and I found I was surprised by my apathy. And so Giancarlo would return to the room, my coffee in his hand, and he would squeeze my arm in his way, but his eyes would be on Laura's eyes, and yet none of it seemed intentional. And in that moment, in that gesture, I saw what it was I could destroy and I stood at the edge, observing my temptation.

It was September and the afternoon streets were full of children in their neat uniforms or wacky t-shirts, the sidewalks crowded by their braids and shoulder bags on my walks. It was at that point my third week in the hostel, and I'd noticed a new ecosystem had begun to open up to me. I'd come to know hostels intimately over the last year, but I'd never stayed in any one longer than about ten days, and I felt something shift after the second weekend turned over, something foundational, the way the new arrivals regarded me, the way the staff suddenly considered me an ally.

The next day was my father's birthday, and I called him early in the evening, when I knew he would be awake in California. He was doing fine, it was the same as every other call I'd made to him in the last few months, he told me about his garden, the oleanders were responding to the gray dishwater he'd begun to save, and how the Kings were playing, never very well, and asked if I'd been visiting a lot of art museums, for years he'd thought I would be a visual artist, something I'd only half-heartedly been interested in in high school, and I told him about the statues I'd seen at the Capitoline museum, where the heads and noses of the pagan-made statues had been smashed in by later Christians in an attempt to erase any proof that they had also been human. He didn't ask when or if I was planning to come back to California, never told me about his weekly visits to my mother unless I asked first. When I came home from Berkeley on college breaks he would always pick me up from the Amtrak station having bought me a vanilla milkshake from In-N-Out, so thick you'd have to use a spoon, and whether I was hungry or cold or not I would consume the whole thing on the way home. We operated this way, my father and I, on signs we'd once decided had meaning, worn tracks of conversation and tradition that neither of us questioned. Of course I felt guilty, at almost all times, for leaving him alone for the last months. I had emailed updates, made sure to call every few weeks, but I didn't tell him, would never tell him, that once I'd left California I felt paralyzed by the thought of going back.

The denial of my request for Vietri's birth certificate arrived around this time, I'd found the envelope tucked into the door of my locker when I returned from a long morning walk. I carried the envelope up to the hostel dorm and then opened it. A short form on official stationery informed me that the record I requested was unavailable. With the opacity of Italian bureaucracy, there was no way to tell if it was unavailable because I did not have permission to request it, because I had not provided enough detail to find it, or because the record did not exist at all. There was no contact to request further information. I was surprised at how quickly I'd received the response, but now the immensity of the roadblock overwhelmed me. I hadn't particularly liked the Hannah Arendt I'd read in college, but one line returned to me now, bureaucracy was tyranny without the tyrant.

If the request had been denied because I'd applied to the wrong location, the wrong commune, I thought I should give up. The only thing I knew was that Vietri had lived in Rome, I had no idea if he'd been born there. If he hadn't, there were over eight thousand communes in Italy, I wouldn't possibly be able to guess his hometown. I lay down on my bunk, the room of twelve beds surprisingly quiet this morning. Usually it was full of nineteen-year-olds hungover and scrambling to make their next flight or train, off to whatever European capital followed on their list. I was suddenly exhausted by the hostel, thought that maybe I should find a room to rent somewhere, but that would admit a desire to stay. I still thought that I might leave Rome at any moment, maybe go to Greece, or Croatia. Even France. I'd never been anywhere else in Europe, I'd barely even been out of Rome. I'd always intended to continue traveling after, if, I'd found Vietri, had a quick visit with my relatives, and now I wondered if I should abandon the search altogether. A room would mean a level of permanency, would mean I should contact my aunts, who would be hurt I hadn't contacted them already. I wondered if Andrea had told them I was in Rome, or if he had kept his promise. So much easier, if they confronted me, to have been night to night in a hostel, a few days in the city to look up an old friend, no time to resume a relationship I'd discarded in my teens, unaware that the tossing away—I always thought of the Italian word, gettare, possibly the origin of the word ghetto, where it's the people who are tossed away—unaware that this rejection might become permanent, that I might one day regret it.

Sometimes when I walked through the city I felt there was a presence behind me. I'd often felt this effect in Rome, had always attributed it in a vague un-thought-out way to its overlapping histories and traumas, empires and populations, it was a city not of ghosts but of shades, and as I walked, sometimes I felt something just behind my left ear, nothing mystical, exactly, but I never felt, even in my long hours of solitude, alone.

Despite this, I was surprised to find on my walks that Rome was an empty city. I hadn't realized it in my previous summers, I'd seldom been moving in a group of less than five family members. Certainly the tourist sites were crowded, I avoided the Colosseum, the Pantheon, any fountain that might have appeared in a Dan Brown novel, but away from them, even in the city center, the streets were empty, though every once in a while I would come across a lone American family darting right and left like a bee that had wandered too far from the hive. I observed something like this to Andrea, who, in his typical fashion, agreed and then went on as if it had been his original observation. It's true, he said, no one lives in those apartments. Half are owned by the church, half by foreign organizations, anything left is for tourists. We all live in the periferia now. After a thought, he added solicitously, you know, we would say, in Romanesco, we would say borgata.

I began to wonder about my mother on these trips. I knew the apartment she'd grown up in, it was my grandparents', the one I'd spent much of my time in during my summers. I knew its large stolid rooms and pale green and yellow wallpapers, the sounds of my aunts' shoes on its tiles, but I didn't know the school she went to, I didn't know her shops and parks, benches and gelaterias. I asked Andrea how often the family got together, now that our grandparents were gone. I was curious about the dynamics, the alliances. He said they didn't see one another very often, my aunt Giulia had left for London, it wasn't like those summers when we had all been young and second and third cousins I'd never heard of had seemed to sprout at family gatherings like mushrooms. Andrea and Clea, I had learned gradually, were the only cousins still living in Rome. Andrea had offered to set something up, and I declined, said maybe later, which, as always, he let pass without comment. I wondered if this was a result of my semi-estrangement from the family, if I was now treated like a skittish animal for whom you might leave food on the porch but don't, at first, try to lure inside. I'd been absent for ten years, lost to them, I thought now, just as my mother was.

I adored Andrea's mother, Settimia, her presence in a room was like a balm to me, everything she seemed to suggest in those family settings was always what I'd been secretly hoping would be decided but was too shy myself to advance. Perhaps it was because Andrea and I were so close in age, and I'd arrived that first summer crucially on the right side of puberty, unembarrassed to receive the affection she showed to both of us, and I was able to keep this ease somehow through the following summers. I was most afraid of seeing her again, of her disappointment that I hadn't seen her immediately, but there was no way to do it, there had never been a single dinner, event, coffee the family in its entirety hadn't been invited to. They took comfort in being around one another in large numbers, like certain flocks of birds or fish. And I knew I hadn't yet faced the vitriol over what had happened with my grandfather before his death, I was still unsure about how they viewed my place in the drama. He'd married the nurse my aunts had hired to look after him as his mind slipped further away from him, had sold the family's apartment and run off to France, and within a year he had died. I'd never been close with my grandfather, by the time I'd started my summers in Rome his mind was seldom present in the room, but the outline of this trauma was still visible in the family ecosystem, and then I hadn't come back for the funeral. I couldn't handle the thought of taking all that on, I knew that I had hurt them with my distance, could tell in everyone's ninety-second share of my annual Christmas call, and I didn't want to face it, I didn't want to own up to the hurt I had caused, to my family and to myself, I wasn't ready to absorb another dozen intimates into my life, my self's private circle. Was it that they weren't truly Romans, that my grandparents had both come to the city from elsewhere, was it a small-village mentality? They clung to one another as a unit and it stifled me, I couldn't imagine my surrender to this loss of autonomy.

It was Giulia, of all of my family, who was the one to insist on sharing my mother's history with me over those teenage summers, but I had hoped to use that time away from California as a break, the rest of the year I went to see my mother every other Sunday morning, awkward visits I dreaded but endured. Giulia was two years older than my mother, though they didn't resemble each other, her hair was a lighter brown, like mine, her body soft, while my mother was dark-haired and built on a wire. She was trying to help, I knew that now, trying to show me the person my mother had been before I'd known her, but I hated hearing these stories. My mother's pregnancy was what had brought on the symptoms of schizophrenia, as long as she had been my mother she had been this new person, and I resented, or felt guilty for, the existence of her old self, the one that perhaps would have continued except for the fact of my conception.

Sometimes I wondered if her pregnancy was accidental, she was only twenty-five when I'd been born, and the thing that had been imparted to me most was her ambition. She'd left Italy at twenty-two to come to Berkeley for a master's degree, a place where she knew no one, and she had only been working at her firm for two years, it was the '80s, she would have known what she had to prove. It was only after my aimless but still disciplined studies that I'd confronted what she'd lost when she disappeared from herself. I'd had to take entrance exams to get into my Catholic high school, then there were the AP classes, college applications, once at Berkeley the papers, the midterms, the finals, the honors thesis, the work, so many hours of work, and I'd studied things I enjoyed, reading-heavy classes that I was already interested in, very little of the graphs and equations I occasionally glimpsed in an open engineering textbook down the table in the library. How could I not have been unwanted, if my mother had known what would happen, how could she have been ready to abandon all of that work?

I felt that I'd done the most reckoning with my upbringing in my teenage years, after I'd stopped my summers in Italy, with friends whose families I could observe objectively. My friends and I felt so distanced from childhood then, so removed with our new bodies, but really we were close enough for the details to be fresh, for the grooves to be vivid. But I was beginning to see how the reckoning would have to happen again and again, every five years, every decade, as the ground shifted beneath my feet and I had to learn to walk again with the knowledge that I had a schizophrenic mother, a great uncertainty that therefore shadowed my own life, that I might become like her, a father I could count on and yet had never felt close to, another web of family six thousand miles away with its own traumas and histories, which I was wary of being drawn into. It was exhausting, why couldn't I set things in place and move on? Why did I keep having these memories, this grief, overwhelm me, often at moments that felt utterly random and therefore unpredictable, not, for example, in front of the ubiquitous depictions of that anguished mother and her child but rather when I smelled a tomato at a vegetable vendor and remembered how my mother would serve them to me after school, on garlic-rubbed toast, with salt and pepper and olive oil.

Chapter Six

I still wanted to find Vietri, I was frustrated I had not accomplished this goal, I'd clung to the scenario for so long, the knock, the chat, the end of my journey, the idea had been so simple. Still, this search didn't consume all of my time, much of it disappeared in the mysterious way that my days of the past months had slipped by, mornings lost to hangovers, afternoons spent reading and walking, excursions to acquire food or views, but it remained a pull at the back of my mind, a question, an unopened box, and every few days I would walk by and test the latch, confirming the continuing fact of my curiosity.

The only thing I knew for sure about him, I thought as I walked, chewing the inside of my bottom lip, the only information I had, other than the list of books he'd bought, was his address. There had never been an email address for him, all his communication with the store had been by letter. He might have given us a phone number, perhaps to provide to the bank, but I wasn't sure, and it would have been too odd to call the store now, who knew who'd be answering the phones, if they'd give out customer information. I'd checked the pagine bianche, hoping to find his phone number in the listings, but not even his name was present. It was funny to me that Italy had a phone book. When, in this country, had anyone ever lost track of a friend or relative, or wanted to contact a stranger? So all I had was the address on the via Bevanda. It would have to be enough.

I had to hope the apartment was in his name, and for the first time I wondered if he'd given us his real name at the bookstore. It occurred to me, as I followed these thoughts, that his real name would have to be used on other things associated with the apartment, for example the electric bill. The utility company could at least confirm this, and I wondered idly what story I could make up if I called, tried to remember if I knew anything at all about utilities in Rome. Surely he would have had an account under his name, the account might even have more than the name, might allow me to fill in more of the taunting blanks on the birth certificate request form.

I tried to ask Andrea about utility setups, calling him later that afternoon at a time when I thought he'd be less likely to be bothered, barely fitting into one of the phone booths at the internet café around the corner, the hostel's pay phones for show, everyone got cheap SIM cards or Skyped on the computers. I asked how complicated they were to set up, which I'd decided was the most plausible way for me to phrase the question. Why? he asked immediately. Are you thinking of renting an apartment? I said something vague and I actually thought I could hear his arm moving in an impatient gesture. But you will probably need a room then, not a whole apartment, Rome is too expensive, in this case you will not need to set it up. I will let you know, he said, as I'd only begun to start protesting, and hung up.

✛   ✛   ✛

I realized I didn't need to go so far as to look up a utility account, really I could check any piece of mail. I tried to remember the dim orange-lit lobby of the apartment building, attempting to summon the memory of a mailbox. I decided that if I was willing to go as far as requesting a complete stranger's birth certificate, if I had possibly stolen and kept in my possession a rare and not unpolitical book from someone named Chiara, then it seemed arbitrary to draw the line at trying to check Vietri's mail. At least, I thought, I should return to the apartment, see if the mailbox was easily accessible, if so, peek at the names, put everything back in its place. A car was exiting the driveway as I walked up the street, I'd timed my visit to the morning, hoping to catch some resident leaving for work, and I broke into a jog, slipping inside the metal gate as it rolled shut, keeping my eye on the car as it continued down the street, but it didn't slow. I doubted they had seen me, given the angle, still, I felt a rush of anxiety, or excitement, as I ascended the stairs, gave three soft knocks on Vietri's door, suddenly afraid of what would happen if the shrill neighbor heard me again. But no one answered, and the steady thuds of my feet moving down the stairs calmed me, by the time I'd returned to the lobby my heartbeat had slowed, my head felt clear. The postboxes were just inside the entryway, thin and metal, with a lock at the bottom so that the door opened upwards to reveal a slot. Vietri's number, like the door buzzer outside, was missing a name card, and I slid my fingers under the lip at the opening and gave it a tug. It didn't move. I looked around to make sure I hadn't been observed, and left the building.

I returned to the apartment building that afternoon at three, that rare quiet hour in Rome. I'd bought, at a tourist stand near the hostel, a heavy metal beer opener, flat, palm-sized, in the shape of the Colosseum. I'd asked the vendor if it was strong and he'd replied fortissima! in an offended tone, and wedged it between two metal postcard displays, using it as a lever to tilt one slightly to the side. I'd smiled and didn't even bother to try to knock half a euro off the price. I entered the lobby quietly, the outside gate caught open an eighth of an inch by a small rock I'd located in the gravel earlier that day, testing to make sure it would open and close without obvious detection. The anxiety of the morning staircase was returning, I didn't know how long Vietri had been gone, if there would be any mail left for him, but there was no point in wasting time, the longer I was there, the greater the chance someone would catch me in the middle of my strange mission, so I walked straight to the box with Vietri's number on it, inserted the bottle opener's edge into the thin slit below the lock, and pushed downwards against it with all of my weight. It didn't give, and I nearly stamped my foot in disappointment. I crouched down until the lock was at eye level. From this angle I could tell the door had given a little, bent now so that there was a thin sliver of white revealed. I inserted the opener again at the crack and brought down the heel of my palm with all of my strength. I felt no hesitation or doubt in this gesture. In my last few years I'd barely influenced, barely touched, barely felt the world, I was so distantly tethered to it I felt in danger of floating away. And now I'd already inserted myself into the narrative of Vietri's life, I wanted to find him, I wanted to prove he existed in reality. The third time I brought my hand down the lock gave with a crack. I reached my hand into the box, took the envelope that lay there, and left the building.

I took the envelope out of my bag only once back at the hostel, feeling too paranoid, or guilty, or superstitious, to examine it on the bus, but my hand had stayed pressed to its shape on the side of my bag as if to feel for a heartbeat. I went into the hostel bar, just opened for the evening, and only then removed it, turning it over to see tree-shaped orange logo of Enel, the energy company, exhaling a breath I hadn't realized I was holding when I saw the name GIORDANO VIETRI. He existed. Vietri was his name. I hadn't admitted to myself how worried I'd been that I would find no trace of him at all, no proof of his existence except my memory, a story that originated and remained only inside of my head, a fear that Vietri was actually a sign that my mind had broken in a fundamental way from the world around me, like I had always feared. He existed, or he had existed.

The bill was three pages, the top of each page listed his name, his address, a customer number consisting of twelve numbers, and something called a codice fiscale, a string of fifteen numbers and letters. No information that would fill in more of the birth certificate request form, but I wasn't bothered, the sips I took of my beer while I scanned through the pages were cheerful and large. I checked the time, almost six. I'd planned a walk with Andrea that evening, and I hurried to finish my beer, secure the envelope in my locker, and dig a sweater out of my backpack, as the evening had turned cool. Andrea met me at the hostel, he had seemed determined to see where I was staying, though we met outside, I hadn't suggested a drink, I didn't want to associate myself in his mind with the hostel bar and the things that happened there.

We walked down toward La Sapienza and then diagonally through the campus, the light beginning to fade, past the small groups of students scattered across the lawns. The patches of grass appeared almost identical to the Californian soccer fields of my childhood, the white starburst of a weed flower, a yellow stumpy thing aspiring to daisy-hood, the dried pine needles like a brown lace overlay on the clumps of green and dirt. I was always surprised by the amount of familiar vegetation in Rome, sometimes I thought it had the flora of California by way of Jerusalem, oleanders and palm trees, the plants of my childhood with those of some Middle Eastern locale, as if I'd had exotic dreams that had unfurled themselves amidst the greenery outside my childhood bedroom window. Everything else had been so different that first summer when I was eleven, the streets, the cars, even the beaches, I'd held this one thing close as if it were for me personally, that the plants could be familiar.

Do you remember that summer at the beach? I asked Andrea. We'd all gone one summer for a few weeks to a coastal town an hour or so south of Rome, all of the aunts and cousins, uncles dropping in for a few days, seeming impermanent and background, as they always did. Andrea had met a girl, or he'd met another group of kids, but really he'd met the girl. She was thin, fifteen to his fourteen, with deep red hair that I might have thought, in other lights, was brunette, but on the beach, in the bright coastal sun, it burned orange. She was fiercely freckled, over almost her entire body, which we saw every day as she and her friends, Andrea with them now, marched their bikinis up and down the sand, the tanned boys in the group following behind with their arms draped over one another or sprinting ahead of the girls like dolphins along the wake of a ship. I was also fourteen that summer, but it seemed she was another age group altogether, I could tell that some invisible membrane separated us. I'd stayed with my younger, more distant cousins, all twelve or eleven, and we laid our bodies out in the sun on display as if hoping someone could walk by and choose us to join this other world.

Andrea has a ragazza, my aunts crooned all night. A girl, a girlfriend, there were only two categories in Italian: it was either ragazza, which simply meant girl, covering any sort of casual relationship, or fidanzata, the same word for fiancée, for an exclusive one, which I thought unremarkable until I myself started dating and imagined having to be in one of the two categories. On one of our last nights on the beach Andrea stayed out later than usual, and in the morning his face and even his neck turned as red as the girl's hair in response to my aunts' crude jokes. I burned with shame for Andrea, and swore to myself that when I was the age to do these things, the next summer, or the one after that, I was sure my breasts would grow sometime, I would never let them catch me.

That sex was so frank in Rome had made me uncomfortable in those years, but now that I was older I respected it, to be able to see a couple in the street and know if and even why they were fucking. I'd never seen such cleavage. Even the girls we passed now on the campus with their oversized shirts and loose imported pants somehow conveyed the outline of their bodies despite the apparent covering. Andrea hadn't answered me, had taken drags on his cigarette as if thinking, and I continued, do you remember that girl? With the red hair? Did you ever see her again? Andrea was giving me a look I couldn't read, as if I were the one to have forgotten an obvious memory. I suddenly felt embarrassed and didn't know why, wanted to change the subject, cast around, and asked, what's a codice fiscale?

He sighed, and rubbed the back of his head, pushing the hair forward, elbow up to the sky. It's like a social security number, he said. We were speaking Italian, which he'd started doing with me since the afternoon he'd introduced me to Giancarlo, and so what he really said was numero sociale, but I knew what he meant. It was endearing to me to hear him speak clumsily, usually he was so precise, and our conversations in Italian put me at the disadvantage, I didn't understand a quarter of the words, felt like I was singing a constant refrain of cosa vuol dire? che cosa vuol dire? Andrea was continuing, talking about taxes. So you get it at birth? I asked. He shook his head. You have one, too, you can figure it out, it's a, and he paused and grimaced, said a word I didn't know. I had an image of him again as a teenager, preoccupied, so much more serious than now, walking hunched over through the apartment, ignoring his mother's calls. But today he brushed it off, told me he'd think of the English word, repeated the Italian one again questioningly. I shrugged. So tomorrow, are you free in the morning? I said yes, unsuspicious. Good, he continued, I have a room for you to look at. It took me a few steps to understand that this room would be for me, a room for me to rent, only then remembered his response when I'd asked how to set up utilities. I'd assumed he'd forgotten. I started to protest, to say I wasn't sure how long I was staying, if I could make the commitment, but he stopped suddenly and smacked the back of his left hand into his right palm. It's an algorithm, he said in English, and only then did I replay the Italian word he'd said, almost identical in spelling, upset I hadn't been able to manage the conversation. I'll send you the calculator, Andrea was saying, so that you can see what yours is.

Later that night I printed out the email Andrea had sent me with the instructions for identifying a codice fiscale, curious now about my own. I looked around for Maria as I entered the hostel bar, though I hadn't seen her since our conversation. I wondered if she'd left the city. I hoped so. I found myself a table, borrowed a pen from the bartender, and began. The first three letters were made up of the consonants of my last name, then those of my first name: MLL GBR. I'd noticed that Vietri's had the familiar *V*'s and *G*'s in his. I looked at the step for the following digits, due numeri per l'anno di nascita, and my breath caught. The next group of numbers were determined by the birth date. I put a coaster on top of my beer, draped my sweater aggressively over my chair to save the table, the bar was reaching the hour where the hordes from the bunks upstairs would gather to pregame, and ran up the stairs to my locker. I returned with the electricity bill with Vietri's number on it. Finally, I would know. I paused, like my boyfriend had pointed out, I had no proof Vietri was old, and I recognized my assumptions were about to be questioned. Was I prepared for Vietri to be my age, or middle-aged and ogling, was I prepared for sex to be on the table? And we were in the tail end of the Berlusconi years, even an advanced age was no guarantee.

Vietri's number was 20T14, and I read the instructions greedily. The first two numbers were the final two of the birth year. So, 1920. The letter code was for the month, December. He was born on December 14, 1920. I had been right, he was old, he'd be ninety-one if he was still alive, just as I'd pictured. I was flooded with a euphoria I hadn't expected to come with this knowledge, though I'd been searching for exactly this, I'd held my emotional investment in the search for Vietri at a distance even from myself. I gave the rest of the instructions only a half glance, ready to channel this excitement into the king's cup game starting at the next table that I'd just been invited to join, but then I saw that the next number was determined by the birthplace. I put down my beer. Andrea had sent me only the instructions for those born abroad, so I went over to the row of computers at the entrance to the bar where I'd printed the original email, fortunately one of them was free, inserted a two-euro coin, and within a few seconds had the page pulled up, the number that identified the commune. I searched for the number in the registry, so excited I mistyped the first time I put in the code. I tried again and there it was: Aliano, the name of the commune, Vietri's birthplace, a town in the Basilicata region. I said the name out loud, its vowels smooth as they exited my mouth.

I logged off the computer, giddy, feeling high on my luck. I had a birth date, I had a hometown. Vietri was his real name. He was a person. One of the king's cup players came over again to ask me if I wanted to join the new round, he was American and bought me two euro beers to bring over so I could catch up. None of the group expressed any curiosity about what I'd been calculating at my table in the corner, what my quick and gleeful Google search was about. I liked that we fellow travelers were so uncurious about the mundanities of one another's days, knew, though, that by the end of the night I was likely to learn things about them that some of their closer friends back home didn't know. Usually I was annoyed by the other Americans in the hostel and tried to avoid them, but this night I felt expansive. The knowledge I'd gained of Vietri made me feel superior in a way none of them would ever understand, and this inequity made me feel in their company lighthearted and unconcerned with the consequences of my actions. We played a few rounds, two, three?, and when the rest of the group left to go out to a club, it was already midnight, the boy who'd first brought me over pulled me into the hallway leading to the dorms and pressed me against the wall. He was younger than me, maybe only twenty-two, was he still in college? I couldn't remember. We found one of the dorms empty and he slid into the bottom bunk next to me and kissed me on the cheek and asked, is this okay? as he wrapped his arms around me and pulled me to him. I nodded, thought it was endearing, this adjusted chivalry after his aggression in the hallway, and then he spooned me for so long I wondered if he did just want platonic companionship, but then the arms around my waist tightened and he pulled me against him, and I felt his erection then, and he began to run his hand up and down my stomach. Is this okay? he asked again, and I nodded and he unbuttoned my top and began to kiss me as his hands traveled over my breasts, and moved on top of me, and I remembered then that he'd mentioned a girlfriend, was only in Rome for a few days, perhaps this caused his hesitation, he ran his hand around the rim of my underwear, and I looked up at him questioningly, I wondered if that was what was making him stop, but I wasn't going to bring it up, and maybe he was drunk and had forgotten he'd told me, but he would move himself so that I could feel how hard he was. Finally he sighed, then took off my underwear, started to kiss down my stomach, positioned himself so that he had turned and was now in my mouth, and began to move his mouth against me so that I had to take all of him in my mouth to absorb the sounds of my moans. His tongue found me, and after I came, I turned around and when short seconds later he filled my mouth, it tasted of salt and slid thickly down my throat, but the name on my lips as I fell asleep was Aliano.

Chapter Seven

The next morning I met Andrea. He'd been so insistent the night before that I'd agreed to look at the room, figuring it couldn't hurt, I'd nod politely at some students and then we'd grab a coffee and that would be it, I'd go on with my morning and the various ways I'd try to fill it. The apartment belonged to a friend of a friend's mother, or something, I hadn't paid much attention to the string of relations, sometimes I preferred to let the stream of Andrea's Italian wash over me without the exertion of trying to figure out every word, I usually got the gist by the end. You'll like this neighborhood, he said as we walked, Parioli is very nice. I looked sideways at him in annoyance, wondering if it was a test. Parioli was one of the most expensive neighborhoods in Rome, surely he knew that I knew that. We passed several gated buildings I was sure were embassies. The door to the apartment building was held open for us by a man in a navy blue uniform, and the lobby of the building was dark, light from the top filtering down faintly, as if Andrea and I stood at the bottom of a deep pool. A small elevator rose up the center, wrapped by a triangular staircase, all brass lines and luxurious creamy yellows. We entered the elevator, barely large enough for the two of us, and I was glad I'd woken up in time to shower and wash my hair, wished I'd remembered to check my neck for marks from the American boy. I hadn't been expecting this luxury. Andrea slid the metal gate closed and pressed four, the highest number. We exited into a space filled with light. There were only two apartment doors on the floor, and he led me to the one on the right, rapped his fingers on the dark wood.

The door was opened by an elderly woman who smiled at us warmly, but with something like exhaustion. I guessed she was in her seventies, her hair was almost purely white, elegantly pulled back, and she wore an orange-and-gold scarf tied over a crisp white shirt. She kissed Andrea first, and then me, and Andrea introduced us, her name was signora Ianucci. Loredana, she added, and she smiled, and I thanked her in formal language for letting us visit. She led us down a hallway to a light-filled room, windows lining the long wall. Old photographs were displayed in silver frames on their sills, and the adjourning wall was lined with bookshelves, a fireplace. The furniture wasn't modern, in fact it was almost ornate, but there was a simplicity somehow to the room, a warmth perhaps brought by the deep red oriental carpets laid over the marble tile, the blue armchairs facing each other convivially, the amount of art and objects showing it had been lived in for a long time. It's beautiful, I said. I was being sincere, it was the most beautiful room I'd ever been in, but I struggled to find the words, il luce, i libri . . . She thanked me, her smile wistful. There was a small kitchen, a terrace. The bedroom itself was bare, just a twin bed and a desk, a long window with a view of the city and the hills beyond covered partly by pine branches.

Do you like it? she asked me, her eyes on my face. Yes, I said, oh, yes.

Out on the street again, I asked Andrea how close his friend was to him, the room should have been much more expensive, I shouldn't have been able to afford it, he'd told me it would be three hundred euro a month before we arrived, which might have made sense if I were sharing an apartment like Giancarlo's with five students in San Lorenzo. Andrea had mentioned in the elevator on the way down that it would be inexpensive because of her age, she doesn't need help, he said, and there's a woman who comes a few times a week to take her to doctors' appointments, prepare some meals, things like that, but it would be good for her to have someone in the apartment with her, just in case. Still, for that neighborhood, the amount was nominal, and I had no experience with the elderly, I thought there must have been something else going on, some other factor, which is why I asked Andrea then how close this friend was to him, though I'd already accepted the room, we'd agreed I would move my things the following Monday, which I'd paid through at the hostel, but Andrea had stopped, was pulling on his cigarette, and he looked me up and down. Was Loredana the mother of his friend, was she doing him a favor? No, he said finally, exhaling. You didn't understand. Her daughter died ten years ago. She's the mother of the best friend of your mother from childhood.

I'd waited until I was back on my bunk at the hostel to burst into tears I couldn't entirely account for, the circuitous order of the Italian words repeating in my head on a loop, la madre, l'amica, la madre. How could I have forgotten, I was in Rome, this was my mother's city.

The next Monday I moved my two bags into the room at Loredana's, grateful I'd had several days to absorb the impact of our connection. That afternoon I went to meet Giancarlo and Laura, where I watched them translate fourteen straight pages of wedding songs and I struggled to identify my emotion as we left, which I finally decided had been a contented boredom. I felt an ease with Giancarlo and Laura, they were peers who were interested in history, in understanding the world and working for good in it. My months of travel had been selfish, pleasure-seeking in nature, and I saw through them, through the connection with Loredana, that it could be different. Laura, on my way out, had caught me by the hand after Giancarlo was already through the door and invited me to a concert with some of her friends the following week, I'd thanked her and tucked the flyer into my bag. I could still feel the way she'd held my fingers in hers, genially, like a Victorian fiancé. Now that I had a room, here was a chance for a community in this city, I saw how a life could build out of this.

Giancarlo and I rode the bus together collegially back toward the city center, one of his roommates had the scooter. He and the others in the apartment had a communal sense of property, none of them were from Rome, and in these post-financial-crisis years they seemed to get by improvisationally, one of them cut all of the others' hair, the scooter wasn't really Giancarlo's but was used between the roommates as the one asset of value, it really belonged to Luca, who was from Milan and seemed to be silently underwriting the activities of the other four. Once I'd suggested we all go out for dinner to Giancarlo and Andrea, and they'd made flimsy excuses, putting me off, I was slowly coming to realize that none of the Italians my age even went out, it wasn't only that they didn't get drunk, that they were capable of drinking one beverage over the course of four hours, it was also they rarely went to bars or restaurants, they didn't have money, I never saw any of them spend any. Once I'd articulated this to myself, I'd felt embarrassed, but couldn't tell if it was on their behalf or mine.

Giancarlo and I spoke of Libya that day, either because we'd been talking about my travels and the various countries I'd been in or, more likely, because NATO was just days away from beginning airstrikes in Tripoli and Brega, Gadhafi only weeks away from being beaten, stabbed, thrown off of a truck, brought dead and semi-naked to a hospital, kept in the freezer of a supermarket for four days before being displayed to the local population, then entombed in a desert funeral at a location that has yet to be revealed.

I was in Libya, you know, Giancarlo had said, and I'd asked him to tell me about it. I went with my friend, Giancarlo said, he is an engineer and the oil company sent him. I got a grant from the university for my ticket. So we go, and you know, the people over there under Gadhafi, he pronounced the name so differently than I'd ever heard that it was only a minute later replaying what he'd said that I understood, so it is very strange, they, the people there, they have a green book which is from the dictatorship, and everyone there, they must read and follow this book. I nodded. There were two young women in head scarves across the aisle from us and a row back, and I grew self-conscious, wondering if they were Libyan.

So my friend, Giancarlo continued, he has his job during the day, and so then, I study Arabic and it's very different there as well, so I am trying to talk to people. I nodded again as the young women got off at the back of the bus. I turned to look at them and noticed only then that one held a baby to her chest. So I am there in a market, Giancarlo said, and I am walking through the stalls, and it is very crowded, so I step aside to something, it's like an alley, and I stand by myself and drink some water. And then I look down and there is an old man sitting there, he is also in the entrance, he is right by my feet but I hadn't seen him there before. I don't know how, maybe he had not moved, maybe I thought he was a pile of clothes, you know his head is covered, so who knows. But he looks up at me and asks if I want to know my future, but I don't understand at first because like I said the Arabic there is very different, so finally I hear it slow and I understand, and so I say of course, why not? And so the old man asks me some questions and I crouch down on the ground with him because like I said it's very loud. And it is very hot and I am drinking water but my bottle is very low, so I am wondering where I can buy more, because, you know, it's better not to drink the water there from the pipes. And he asks me my mother's name, and when he opens his mouth, I see that he has only a few teeth, in the very back, and I am thinking about his teeth and water and my mother and then he asks how old I want to be when I get married. And it was on this trip, well, Laura and I were fiancés officially, we were going to get married maybe that summer, maybe the next one. And before I can answer the man grabs my pants by the pockets and he asks me for money, only the price he says is, pfff, ridiculous, and I realize there's something wrong with his brain, he's not just trying a scam, you know, otherwise he would have told me the fortune first and then said I couldn't take it back, and I look into his eyes for the first time and I become a bit frightened even though it's not rational. So I try to stand but he still has my pants by the pockets, and he is strong, and for a moment he lifts off the ground, just this much, and falls back to the ground. And I run away, I don't know why, but I go back to the hotel and I call Laura and I tell her we cannot get married.

He looked at me with a sheepish, conspiratorial smile, heartbreaking to me in its certainty that I had understood. But I hadn't understood anything at all.

The next afternoon I was reading in the Villa Borghese when a rainstorm started. I'd only just been in the apartment, Loredana and I had eaten lunch together, and I didn't feel ready to go back. I felt awkward, it was her house, and I tended to my old schedule of the hostel, locked out during the afternoon hours and wandering the city during that time. As Andrea had told me, there was a girl who came, a Polish girl a few years older than me named Agnieszka, as well as Demba, a Senegalese man who stopped by once a week or so to take care of handyman-like tasks, and I disliked the feeling that I might be interrupting their routines, had a deeply American discomfort with the idea of hired help, which I reacted to by trying to avoid any proof of their existence. So instead of making my way back to the apartment, I bought a cheap umbrella from a vendor on the side of one of the paths and descended the steps from the height of the park. I looked around at the bottom of the stairs, usually crowded with families posing with their gelato cones, standing still as the rain fell around the umbrella and the water traveled down, as the violent drops disrupted the surface of the fountain. To my left was a small wooden sign timidly announcing the presence of the Keats-Shelley museum. I didn't particularly feel the need to escape the weather, but I wasn't so unsuggestible as to want to stay in the rain. More than anything what led me inside the large wood-paneled doors to pay my twelve-euro fee was not any scholarly interest but instead a sudden craving to be surrounded by English words, to forget the bureaucratic Italian that had lately occupied my thoughts, the twisty Arabic translations, my stilted, polite conversations with Loredana and Agnieszka, who spoke slightly more Italian than I did and less English than that.

In college, earnestly, I'd decided to take all of my courses for the English major in chronological order, and after Chaucer, Spenser, early picaresque comic novels that meandered through the English countryside that I was unable to find even the least bit funny, after those texts the Romantics had felt like a new window. It wasn't exactly that I loved their poetry, even in nature-worshiping California I had found their reactions to mountain peaks overwrought, but I did have a respect for their values, I'd felt a kind of kinship with them. As I moved through the stately dark-paneled rooms of the museum, chairs arranged politely with their backs against the walls, I was drawn most to the story of Percy and Mary Shelley. Their movements around Italy were erratic, frequent, four years in the country and nowhere longer than a few months, a story full of elopements, tuberculosis, drownings, all by the time she was twenty-five. But the story in the glass cases turned, and I read horrified about the trail of dead infants they'd left across this country, one baby died in Mary's arms in the hallway of an inn where Percy was searching for a doctor; a mysterious child was adopted and then left in Naples, herself dead within two years; another child's death was attributed mysteriously to "moving," as if the fact of her parents' restlessness had weakened her own hold on life. Then one afternoon Percy went out in a boat in the bay near Venice, and within a few hours was overswept by a storm, his body taking ten days to reach the shore. All of their years were a risk, and I wondered at their choices, wondered at what point movement for movement's sake was no longer worth the sacrifice, I thought again of Maria. But I identified with the Shelleys, I looked at their portraits as I left the museum with an unexpected nostalgia, they seemed to know that stopping was its own kind of death.

The rain had cleared and the streets were now crowded

with Romans lurching home in their tiny cars, and as I walked, I turned deliberately into the emptier ones, having to double back several times when they dead-ended into alleys, but I needed to be away from the pushing and noises, my chest was full of emotion I wanted to disperse. Suddenly the room at Loredana's felt like a trap, I felt stifled, panicked. My thoughts spiraled, and I knew that the book of the Palestinian village couldn't have had anything to do with Vietri. It was a red herring, whoever this Chiara was, whatever I'd said to the barman to make him give the book to me, we'd by now translated enough of it that I couldn't imagine how it was Vietri's, it approached him asymptotically, I felt sure that there would be no ultimate connection. My search for Vietri would dead-end like those alleys, and then what was I still doing in Rome, what was this life I thought I was living? I wandered, agitated, this way for an hour or more, erratically south, until the sun was setting and I realized what it was I wanted to do. It was freedom that I still wanted, but then I had always tended to covet exactly the wrong thing.

Chapter Eight

I woke up in Giancarlo's apartment, his roommates noisy outside the door, the room bright and cruel. He was no longer in the bed next to me, but his cell phone's buzz had woken me up. Without giving myself time to stop, I checked it, and the small gray screen showed a message from Laura. Once I'd opened one of Laura's books to an inscription from Giancarlo, barely legible because of his small, cramped handwriting, the Italian full of jokes and abbreviations I didn't fully understand, and it had occurred to me that this was what real intimacy would look like, a fully formed culture created between two people, a circle including just them. I didn't read the message on the phone screen, instead I dressed quickly. I liked Laura, I thought. But I'd known exactly what I was doing the night before. I wanted to get out as soon as possible, before Giancarlo came back from wherever he was, mostly likely the bathroom, so I found my bag, dressed quickly, and opened the door, almost running by the doorway to the living room, where I could see Giancarlo's roommates and maybe Giancarlo, but I didn't look directly, just ran, now, out of the building, noticing as I did the enormous claws of the garbage truck cranes, shaped like a tulip's petals, and the rounded forms of the dumpsters themselves, in their preschool colors, like the limbless creatures of some kinder planet.

I snuck into Loredana's apartment quietly, exhaling only when I closed the door to my room, grateful I hadn't run into her or Agnieszka wearing yesterday's clothes, wondering if my absence the night before had been noticed. I lay on the bed, rubbing my face with both hands. Every thought, every physical sensation, filled me with dread. I had taken Giancarlo to an Irish bar full of tourists, had bought us round after round of gin and tonics. I had been sick of these buttoned-up Italians and their total control, I had wanted to see him loose, to push him into my arena, where the weapons were familiar. I supposed it had worked, had only the haziest memory of us supporting each other on the way back to his apartment, of the condom wrapper being tossed to the floor, of his sloppy expression as he came. I spent the entire day in bed, dozing on and off, grateful I had my own bathroom in which to vomit, spooning a pillow in my misery.

What was I doing in Rome? I hadn't even seen my family. The call of endless motion had seemed so strong to me the night before, I had wanted to return to my routine of South America, shedding an old self as I left city after city. I knew that was why I had sought out, had slept with Giancarlo, this destructive tic was familiar to me, I'd done it to force myself to leave Rome. It was the same reason I'd cheated on my boyfriend I'd lived with in Oakland, it was to burn the bridges to this city, so that I would leave before I had the chance to get ensnared into a life.

Sometimes, in recent weeks, I had had the thought that 10 percent wasn't that much. It wasn't as huge as I had believed when I was twenty. But then if my life did continue, what did I have to show for my years? A life I'd destroyed for a few months of travel, and a failure to find an old man I had never met. The shape of my years since college was so unclear to me, I even found it difficult to answer when people asked me what place I had liked best from my travels. I panicked every time and gave a different answer, usually with the same explanation: it's beautiful, and the food! But what was wrong with me that I'd now seen the better part of another continent and I couldn't name a place I liked best, could only think of the eucalyptus groves on the bottom of the Berkeley campus, hundred-year-old trees with enormous twisting trunks where they usually found at least one suicide every year, hanging placidly among the branches. But these trees had always given me a feeling of peace, though I was supposed to hate eucalyptuses as a Californian, they'd been planted shortsightedly by settlers because they grew fast, but their wood was too splintery to build with, instead their leaves dropped oil that killed native species and contributed to the hill fires every October. But I couldn't help it, I loved the trees in that grove around the creek, their leaves curved and elegant, reaching for the ground like thousands of elderly fingers. But this wasn't really a place, it was a feeling, and one I'd been far away from for a long time.

That evening I heard a knock on my door, and Loredana's voice asking if I would like to join her for a cup of tea. I'd been sleeping all day in sweatpants and a messy ponytail, but something about the formal phrasing of her request made me decide to change. I washed my face carefully in the shower, removing the mascara of the day before. I put on a raw silk top I'd bought from a Nepalese woman in Buenos Aires, the fabric soft but the stiff collar lending a bit of dignity, which I needed. I sat on the edge of the sofa, Loredana already perched with her antiquated posture in an armchair, and I resisted the urge to curl my feet up underneath me, to wrap myself into a ball. Loredana and I had only exchanged pleasantries while I was on my way in or out in the week and a half I'd occupied the room, had had a few small conversations during the handful of lunches we had shared. I had spent most of the days outside of the apartment or else in my room, unable to escape the feeling that the apartment was hers, and that I was intruding, knowing, also, this distance was so that when I left it would be easy.

Loredana handed me a cup of tea with a small smile, and asked if I was hungry. I shook my head, not lying, but dinner was funny here, unpredictable, I remembered once one of my aunts had offered me a single fried egg for the meal. The tea was very hot, but the first sip, chamomile, was immediately soothing to my stomach.

I wanted to tell you about my daughter, she began cautiously, and paused. I leaned forward and did my best to give her a small smile that I hoped wasn't strained. Of course I'd been curious, but I could feel my heart rate increasing, even after all this time, I realized I'd been hoping she might never tell me, I still preferred to not learn about my mother as she'd been before. I took a deep breath, focused on letting it out of my body as slowly as possible. It was very difficult for me to conceive, Loredana began. She spoke with simple words, in a measured pace, as if her main aim was for me to understand her word by word, and not the larger meaning. When Benedetta was born, I was so grateful. She smiled. My husband was a very good man, but his family did not like me. I'm afraid they saw me as northern, cold. The town I came from was very small, so close to the border I'm not sure they even considered me Italian. They are still upset that I am in this apartment, as if I should have been removed when my husband passed away. I'm afraid they extended these feelings to Benedetta as well. Her grandparents openly preferred her cousins. The children picked up on this, of course, and used the information in a cruel manner. My husband would try to shield her from the worst, but they were his family, we still saw them frequently. I so badly wanted Benedetta to have a sibling, but the doctors had told me it would be very difficult, with some complications that had happened during her birth. She took a long sip of tea. We were not granted another child. I was so grateful for your mother. They were friends from almost the first day of school. Your mother was so full of light as a child, she invested Benedetta with some of it as well. The change was immediate, as if all Benedetta had been waiting for her whole, short life was a peer to tell her she was worthy. She even grew five centimeters that year. They used to come here every day after school, your mother said she liked the quiet. She had her sisters, her house was very loud, though I know for that reason Benedetta loved it there, and sometimes your mother would agree to go there since she knew Benedetta wanted to. They were the type of little girls who would stand as close together as possible, they always seemed to be whispering in each other's ears and clutching each other by the arm. Most days they were here, and I would make them a little snack and they would play right there, she gestured to the space under the large window where the family pictures were arranged. I feel like most of their childhoods passed in this room.

You mother had a difficult time in middle school, Loredana continued. She became tempestuous, but they remained just as close. They would come in from school and I would hear your mother crying angrily, sometimes she even lashed out at Benedetta. I've wondered since then if this was a sort of . . . premonition, of the darkness that was to come. She was so moody, it wasn't like anything I or my friends had experienced at that age. I noticed suddenly there were tears on my face, the silk of my sleeve darkened as I removed them. I was grateful when Loredana did not mention them.

All of that changed when the girls were fifteen, she continued. One day when Benedetta's father was leaving his office a man he had never met walked right up to him and shot him, once in the head and twice in the chest. They call it an assassination, but he was murdered. It wasn't an assassination, that makes it sound noble, for a purpose. He didn't have anything to do with politics.

Things changed again between them after that. There was

some ugliness, like I said, with my husband's family over this apartment. Benedetta changed completely. Now it was she who grew silent. She never cried, not after the first week, but she didn't leave the apartment for a month. Sometimes I would find her standing, staring into space, not at anything at all. When I would come upon her, she would move as if she had only paused for a moment, but I could see the sadness of her early childhood returning, I felt powerless to stop it. Now your mother became again full of light, as if the two girls always needed to stay in balance. It's only because of her that Benedetta returned to school, your mother appeared at the apartment one morning and ensured that it happened, though Benedetta continued to move as if underwater. I'm sorry to say that I hadn't noticed how long the absence had gone on. My grief was very hard to bear, you know. My husband was all the family I had, until Benedetta.

Your mother dragged Benedetta through her adolescence, I think only with the force of her own will. Benedetta tried to kill herself, the first time, when she was sixteen, and your mother lived here for months afterward, slept with her in her bed, refused to leave her side. By the time they started university things were better, they both stayed in Rome and saw each other frequently, though they were in different courses at different universities, they would still study together, often at this table. I know your mother was nervous about leaving her to go to the States for her graduate studies. But they were now twenty-two, and though Benedetta was never the same, she carried her sadness throughout these years, she was much better. She wanted your mother to go, wanted to visit her in California.

Benedetta was at your parents' wedding, and when you were born, when your mother had her problems, she went over to try to help. But she came back quickly, she didn't feel there was much she could do. She could only visit your mother for an hour a day, and you were just a baby. It was very hard for her, that visit. She had some good years after that, she was engaged for a while to a nice boy, she liked her work, she designed things on the computer for companies, but I'm not sure she ever recovered from losing the support of your mother. Even after she got out of the hospital, it was like your mother didn't recognize Benedetta's voice on the phone, she would tell me. It became too painful for her to call. She died ten years ago, she had some problems over the years, terrible boyfriends, but when she died it was intentional. Anyway, these are just the things I thought you might want to know. I have a few boxes of her things, Benedetta's, some clothes and school papers and photos, and there's a lot of your mother in there, if you would ever like me to show you.

In my bed that night, I realized for the first time in years I wanted to talk to my mother. There was information only she knew, had the two friends kept in touch throughout my childhood, had Benedetta been a presence that I'd forgotten? There had been cards and gifts that arrived for me from Italy on my birthdays, but I was a greedy child, my mother had so many relatives I'd never met, I never bothered to remember who had sent them. But now I wanted to know more about this fable that had ended so terribly for both little girls, wondering if it would ever stop, this tally of ways we had lost my mother.

The last time I'd seen my mother was on my twenty-fifth birthday, the last one I'd had before leaving California. I'd driven myself to her residential home in a nondescript suburb of Sacramento. Ever since I'd gotten a driver's license at sixteen I'd visited her alone, continuing every other Sunday during middle school and high school, on every visit home from college after I'd left for Berkeley. Her eyes were unfocused, the light in them had dimmed, and somehow I could tell she had not been the one to brush her own hair. When I remembered the years of my childhood, I remembered the terrors of her mood swings, the volatility of life when we shared a home, the episodes that stalked the edges of my memory. But I also remembered her sharpness, how she could cut to the quick on things, whether it was in helping with my homework or analyzing the lazy neighborhood gossip. In my childhood I'd frequently caught my father giving her a frankly admiring look, and I could see how even casual acquaintances valued her wit, her intelligence. My mother's sentences, at least when she was taking her recommended prescriptions, were always short and clipped, she exerted control over each syllable that left her mouth. Nothing was more important to her than her own intelligence.

She moved uncertainly, she said her medications made

her dizzy, so when she was not sitting rigid in her chair, she moved like a small child just learning to walk, or a creature of the ocean floor, arms spread wide, motions fluid but uncertain. She had always been a careful dresser, wary of her figure, but since she'd gone to live at these facilities, she appeared to me in grays, her face and body bloated from the starches and lack of exercise. A tremor affected the bottom left quadrant of her mouth, and I remembered watching it on that afternoon, transfixed, braced for its next spasm as if for the aftershock of an earthquake. Other than this movement, though, her body was incredibly still, she sat straight in her chair across the table from me, her hands on both armrests of the chair as if strapped. I wondered if they ever were. My father had several times tried to tell me about the research he'd done into the places she stayed, how things were progressive and they didn't do, he said carefully, things that had been done before to people like my mother, things I saw he couldn't bring himself to tell me about, anyway things that might still have been done in Italy, so it was better she was here, he'd tried to explain this to her sisters, but I was already changing the subject because I didn't want to hear, only wanted to leave the room and scream somewhere, but how could I, it was the suburbs, so instead I would hold my book closer to my face and put my iPod earbuds in. How grateful I'd been to the iPod in high school, the comfort of its white earbuds and their power to exclude the world. And so I would wait, wait until my father stopped talking about the things that were and were not happening to my mother while the words in my ears and the words on the page swam together into an incomprehensible soup, and I wondered, sometimes, if this is what it had felt like, those early years when she was changing.

Nothing in particular had happened on this last visit, though my father had, in his tentative way, tried to ask me several times. I knew he thought she'd said something sharp and cutting, as she had so often before, maybe he even imagined she'd had a violent episode of some sort that had been kept from him. I didn't know how to tell him that I'd have preferred that, that nothing at all had happened, nothing except that I'd sat in a room with my mother for an hour on my last birthday, and during this hour I felt nothing but a grief so overwhelming I decided it no longer made sense, I no longer wanted this life I'd been given. And so I'd never gone back, I'd left the country two months later.

I'd known then that it was a terrible thing that I'd done, to have left her that way, but in a different way from how I knew the fact now. I was also old enough to realize that it didn't matter that I knew it, that it was terrible, what mattered was that I had done it, and that I would never be able to explain it to her sisters.

Chapter Nine

The next morning I woke up with the knowledge that what had been tugging at the back of my mind was the name of the town where Vietri had been born. Aliano. I hadn't thought about Vietri among the events of the previous days, ready as I'd felt to leave Rome. But the town, I knew that morning as I lay in my narrow bed, as the green tops of the Seussian pines waved casually out the window, as my unformed thoughts crawled their way toward consciousness, I knew the name of the town was familiar.

I got out of bed and wrapped a soft robe around myself—a gift from Loredana, I'd found it neatly wrapped on my bed a few days after moving in—and went into the study and sat in front of the computer there. This was my favorite room in the apartment, with its dark shelves, long windows, and dusty, heavy smell. Loredana's husband's collection of books was quite large, the kind, I assumed, amassed over generations of inheritances, and judging from the shelves he'd been particularly interested in the Greek and Roman classics, there were beautiful editions that I had yet to open for fear of cracking the spines. As with all rooms full of books, there was a unique kind of silence, cushioned by the bound paper lining the walls, and I felt reverent as I shut the door softly behind me. Loredana rarely entered this room, I'd noticed, but she'd encouraged me to use it as often as I wanted, had seemed quietly pleased by the idea. There was an enormous oak desk that dominated the space, its surface bare, while the desktop sat in a corner on a small stand, plastic, beige, and conspicuous. I'd been surprised that Loredana owned a computer, but I supposed at some level of wealth technologies were acquired rather than sought out.

The connection was slow, but once Google loaded I typed in the name of the town, and there it was, Aliano, the setting of a well-known prewar memoir I'd read excerpts of in college. Written by a communist painter who'd been sentenced for his anti-fascist activities, the book chronicled the two years of his exile there. It was well-known in Italy, I remembered that at least some of my cousins had had to read it in school. The part I'd read, I tried to remember as I rocked back in the chair, concerned the plight of the peasants under the fascist state, it was for a class called something like Reckoning with the Trauma of the Twentieth Century, taken to satisfy one of Berkeley's world history requirements. The course materials had ended up such a catalog of horrors around the globe, trenches in France, famine in South Asia, death camps, gulags, that it was hard for anything distinct to remain clear in my memory. I thought I remembered a scene when the fascist government had raised the taxes on livestock, and the peasants, already entrenched in a cycle of debt and near starvation and unable to come up with the cash, were instead forced to slaughter their goats. They'd feasted for a week, many of their children had never tasted meat, and after were left without milk or cheese or any source of protein, their diet reduced to a hard black bread made once a week in enormous loaves, so tough the practice was to cut it toward the body while girding it against the stomach. The graduate student who'd taught my discussion section had treated the absurdities and inefficiencies of the fascist state as hilarious, but I remembered only being able to find them tragic.

After a thought, I googled the author's name along with Vietri's, then Vietri's with the town, but there were no relevant results.

An English copy of the book was easy to find, I walked down through the clean leafy streets of Parioli to the enormous three-story bookstore at the Termini station and found two copies on the shelf, remembering as I moved among the other travelers that first afternoon I'd arrived in Rome. It occurred to me that I was beginning to glimpse another Rome, one I wasn't sure I'd been aware of when I was fifteen and homesick for the dry, golden California summers.

At a store across from the station I bought a cell phone with preloaded minutes. I thought it would be good to have in case Loredana needed to reach me in an emergency, she had mentioned a heart condition, and in a world without her daughter, I decided that it was a small thing that I could give, what I could offer her was my presence. I entered the phone number of the apartment into the phone from the page where I'd written it in my notebook, and after a moment of hesitation I entered Andrea's as well, then texted him so that he would have the number. I would not be leaving Rome, not yet.

I went next to a café I'd found a street or two off of the Piazza Navona, in the middle of the rounded bump poked by the river into the west of the city. The piazza's Bernini fountain had in fact been featured in a Dan Brown novel, and the café was filled with British tourists thrust onto the sidewalk on tables the size of prayer mats, but the very good glasses of wine were two euro and I liked that I'd found it, that it was mine. It was a relief to be away from the divey student places near the Sapienza, the silent luxury of Parioli. I liked to return to the anonymity of being a tourist, to be exempt from all of the silent rules governing my behavior when I was among Italians, to be able to order a glass of wine without a meal, to have it expected that I would not even try to speak Italian. Giancarlo and Laura had been the last people to speak to me in English, now that I'd so expertly severed that tie, and moved out of the hostel, it would be only Italian, Loredana and Andrea both spoke it with me exclusively, offering a word if I seemed stuck, Loredana hesitantly, Andrea impatiently.

I read the memoir over the spread of the afternoon. It was short, episodic, made up of vignettes describing the notable inhabitants of the village: his landlady, a known witch; the barber, her lover and a violent albino; the petty fascist officials, unoccupied and largely ignored. The town had been carved into a hillside of white clay in a region renamed after a forgotten Byzantine emperor, perched as the Lucanian Apennines crumbled jaggedly toward the high arch of the peninsula. The painter was in jail in Milan before his sentence was reduced to exile, and he first finds the village a paradise, and then another prison. At sundown, once the heat of the day has faded, the town's inhabitants gather in small clumps to gossip in the piazza, a stretch of packed dirt lined by a low wall at the top of the stairs leading down the steep hillside farther into the valley. The major fascist contribution to the village, a large public toilet, set as if it were a monument in the main square, was primarily used by various domesticated, unpenned animals in search of shade and moisture. Occasionally young boys attempted to prove their courage by leaping off the stone roof onto the hard ground three meters below.

According to the painter, peasants regarded the fates of the political prisoners as similar to their own, some being, in some other place, made a decision on a whim, and here they all were. I stopped on the line "They don't consider themselves human beings, like the people in Rome." How could they, one of them dies of a burst appendix, his cries echoing down the mountain, his family unable to afford the useless, nearly blind village doctor. Children don't play in the streets, instead they lean, listless, in the town's short shadows, bellies distended from malnutrition and skin turned yellow by malaria, they beg not for money or candies but for quinine pills.

But reading the book in whole, I found it wasn't only a catalog of these medical horrors, the painter's observations are full of wonder and melancholy as he wanders day by day from the cemetery at the top of the town to the last house at the bottom, the limits of his freedom, and I thought it cruel that my professor had chopped it so mercilessly into parts for the class. I had a superstition about books then, that they should always be respected as whole entities, it was painful to me in college to read fifty assigned pages photocopied into a course reader. I'd never abandoned a book I'd started, it felt like I was leaving a soul incomplete. It would take me years to break the habit, and when I did there would be a sense of loss, as if my soul, too, was less complete having abandoned this practice.

The memoir ended with the political prisoners being freed in celebration of the Italian army's victory in Ethiopia, the painter says his goodbyes and leaves the village. But I knew, or I thought I remembered, that there was a tragic ending not contained in the book. The painter wrote nothing of his life before his exile, only the short biographical note on the back of the book told me he'd been born in Turin. I was curious about him, there was so little truly personal information in his book, everything was outward-facing, focused on his observations of the present moment. I wondered what he'd done to be arrested, what had happened to him after he was freed. The bio noted that he'd died in 1943, nearly seven years after his release. And never once in the memoir was it mentioned, by himself, the fascist officials, the peasants, or the village gossips, never once was it mentioned that the painter was Jewish.

I'd done the math before I started reading: Vietri had been born in 1920, and the painter was kept in the village from 1935 to 1936. It was possible they'd met, even that Vietri could be mentioned in the memoir, the town had less than two thousand inhabitants, but the painter had taken care to note at the beginning of the text that all of the names had been changed.

There were no English-language biographies of the painter, and the Wikipedia page was sparse, barely more information than the bio on the back on the book, listing his death in 1943 in a town I located on the Swiss border, near Lake Como. The Italian biography was already two decades old, but I found it for sale at the third bookstore I tried, in a student-frequented place in San Lorenzo near a café where I'd often met Andrea. It surprised me that there was no more recent biography, given the popularity of his memoir, but it seemed to me that his book was now only read by schoolchildren to learn lessons about the extremity of southern poverty and the hardships of the past, or, I supposed, by tourists passing through the Termini curious about some bucolic recollection of scenic villages, soon to be surprised. I thought of his description of the long sad eyes of the village dogs, the fierce expression of the black Madonna when the statue was unveiled in the street on her feast day. The book deserved better.

I spent the weekend reading the biography, the language dense and circuitous in the manner of the global academy, so that at times I would realize that my eyes had traversed entire pages without absorbing anything, only the repetition of certain words, stato, fascismo, Torino, sorella. It was clear to me how far I was from being fluent in Italian, despite how smoothly I could get through the five-line transactions that made up most of my days, my childish conversations with Andrea and Loredana. I found myself returning to the translation of the memoir as I read the biography out of a craving for simple clear prose in my own language, and the weekend passed, back and forth between the English and the Italian, the first person and the third, the translated and the unsullied, the village and the world.

The painter had been raised in Turin in a comfortable home. His family's roots in the city ran deep, his father owned a steel factory on the outskirts, and he and his sister, elder by four years, were given expensive, coddled educations. He was just barely of the generation young enough to have escaped the First World War, if it had gone on another year he would have turned twenty and been sent to the front. They, those of his birth year, were called the line of '98, his cousin, born nine months before him, was killed in a tunnel carved recently into a mountainside by a canister of tear gas dropped neatly by the Austrians from above. The war had ended, he'd enrolled in the university to study chemistry, Italy's territory gains from the war amounted to a few villages, one or two scenic peaks, and how, then, could he concentrate on his studies, the hallways had gone silent before him. After two years he'd wandered away from its disciplines, replacing the clean, sharp smells of the chemistry lab with the sticky-thick fumes of oil paints, the hiss of the burner with the crack of dried canvas across a boarded frame. He went to Paris for almost a year, returned to Italy, and spent most of his time in his family's summer home on the coast of Liguria. He painted. An arbitrary line had been drawn, and he'd fallen on the right side.

I had made it only halfway through the biography when I grew impatient, I wanted to know more about the painter and his strange, short life, this was my problem with my life as well, I wanted to know the ending. I searched for other publications on the painter on Google Scholar, which led me to an article on JSTOR published by a doctoral student at Roma Tre, on the painter's reputation abroad in the postwar years, particularly in Germany and America. I'd found the author of the article's name in the directory of Roma Tre, and it was as simple as writing her an email that said I had read her article, that I had an interest in the painter and I would love to buy her dinner, lying only a little when I said I was from Berkeley and implying an adjacent scholarly interest of my own.

Even though I'd given him my cell phone number, I'd avoided Andrea for a week or so after the spectacular way I had ended my friendship with Giancarlo and Laura. That night, Giancarlo had placed his hand tenderly between my head and the wall, I had put my fingers under his long, soft lashes and, stroking up, had asked if he knew what a butterfly kiss was. I knew I had ruined something there, but I wasn't sure precisely what it was. In any case, I was grateful my actions didn't seem to have filtered to Andrea, or perhaps they had and he had decided to ignore it, whichever it was, he never mentioned Giancarlo or Laura to me again.

I had realized, after the absence of a week, that I enjoyed Andrea's company, it was a surprise, even a revelation, to have his friendship. He was observant and cynical, it was fun to bring up a topic and watch his thoughts unspool. I told him about the dinner I'd set up with the scholar who had written about the painter, and he asked when it was, and I said in a few days. Anna, the woman I was meeting, had written that she was likely to return to Sardinia in the next month, and graciously, I thought, arranged her schedule so that we would be able to meet before then. Ah, Andrea said. You will have to talk first, then, she's a Sardinian. And then, in response to my expression, offered, well, Sardinians, they are quiet, and went on to expound on the nature of Sardinians, inserting occasionally, as if he'd registered my skepticism, the phrase these are stereotypes, you know they're not all true, before repeating generalizations, gossip, and anecdotes of each of the three or four Sardinians he'd ever met in his life. My feelings were equally divided between three reactions to this speech: I was annoyed, deeply, at his bombast, I was also genuinely touched by his desire to prepare me for the meeting, and I was awed, an emotion I did not normally associate with Andrea, at how sincerely he believed this geographical fact of her birth would determine how the two of us might get along at dinner. My Roman family's casual racism had been bewildering to me as a teenager, and I had never decided if this expansion of prejudice beyond the boundaries of nationality or skin color to nearly the village level made it better, or if it made it worse.

✣   ✣   ✣

When I arrived at the restaurant, Anna was already seated at a table along the sidewall adjacent to the door. Her face was thin and pale, her dark hair pulled tightly back, she was several years older than I was but trying to seem even a few more. She stood to greet me, shaking my hand instead of kissing me, and gestured for me to take a seat. English? she asked, and I replied in Italian that either was fine. She grimaced slightly and began to speak in English. I had expected her to be curious about my interest in the painter, but she didn't even ask what it was I wanted to know. Instead, she launched into a description of her studies as if giving me a résumé, her laureate in Pisa, her dottorato at Roma Tre. She was now in search of a university position, she concluded, a search that was now entering its second year. Most of her colleagues had gone to the States, or to England, but there was very little interest in her subject outside of Italy, or even in Italy, she shrugged. She'd been hoping to find a position in Turin, but the academics there were, she made a gesture, the fingers entwined with those of the opposite hand to make a solid sphere of digits, which she then shook. Her parents owned a farm still in operation in the interior of Sardinia that they'd turned into an ecotourism bed-and-breakfast, and her siblings and their spouses all lived there now, along with the rotating presence of foreign travelers. Soon she might have to go back while she looked for a placement, she said, as she had mentioned in our correspondence.

Who knows if anything will work out, she shrugged, looking past my shoulder as she precisely cut the last tomatoes of the summer and took a small sip of her wine. She wasn't warm at all, I hated the thought that the things Andrea had told me were largely right, but she possessed a directness and an air of fatalism that made me like her.

Anna had written her dissertation, she continued, on the Torino Sei, a group of painters, including mine, as she referred to him, who had debuted together at the Venice Biennale at the end of the 1920s. They were all from Turin, of varying backgrounds and visual styles, christened by this geographical accident and bonded by their shared youth, they had all been young enough to miss the war. They embraced their status as a group, my painter had invited them all to his family's villa on the coast of Liguria, a stay intended only to last for a few weeks of the summer months, but they'd all ended up living there for nearly half a decade. They'd created a community, isolated from the outside world, and devoted themselves wholly to their work. The villa had been intended as a summer residence, it was impossible to heat in the winters, three seasons of the year were so damp that they all lost several works on canvas to mold, but there were orchards, there was the ocean, there was the north-facing, constant light in the rooms in which they painted. Their nicknames for one another were numbers, based on their assignments at that fair. One of them, Gian Luca, Secondo, brought his wife and newborn son, some of them had mistresses who were there for months or years, Gian Luca's wife had another child, at least three of them were one another's lovers at one point or another over those years. It was utopic, they lived totally communally, taking turns bicycling into town for food supplies paid for by money they received sporadically from relatives, or, less often, when one of them sold a painting. In the summer they ate the fruit from the orchards, in the fall they harvested the olives and made their own oil. They all painted the same things, the villa, the women, the children, the olive orchards in harvest, the waves of the ocean after a storm, but their styles remained distinct, perhaps because of the proximity they guarded their borders closely. Their outputs were enormous during those years. Anna took a long drink of her water.

It's not that they were unaware of the political movements happening, how could they be, they were all from Turin and would return to visit their families, of course they noticed the men walking through the streets with pistols and black arms. But they believed in reacting aesthetically, rejecting the classical grandeur of futurism, the metaphysical painters with their spooky piazzas, they were after what they called a pictorial language of freedom. They believed that there was no choice between art and politics, that the way to oppose fascism was through their art. Our plates were cleared, the left-behind juices of the tomatoes slipping on the oil like beads of blood. I wanted to ask Anna what one painted in a pictorial language of freedom, but did not.

My painter would return to Turin for all of the holidays, she continued, and his parents would come to spend weeks in their villa in the summer, the group all loved his mother especially. She sat for portraits for all of them, but she would never admit to liking any of them, she referred to them as the fools in the castle. His father was more tolerant, his mother would say that she had to care about respectability since she was the only one who would. Every time she visited she would pull aside Gian Luca's wife and give her a lecture on the risks of bringing a child up in such an environment, and Marta, a Slovene, would smile back with her broad, placid Slavic face. But you can see his mother's fondness for all of them in her eyes in the paintings they made of her, Anna added. When his mother died, the painter was thirty-four and his friends carried him all the way to the beach on their shoulders and threw him into the ocean fully clothed. Her death was the beginning of the dissolution of their group.

He returned to Turin for the funeral, had only been gone from the villa for three weeks when he received another telegram, Gian Luca had died. Tuberculosis. He'd had the cough so long they'd stopped noticing. My painter returned for the second burial in as many months.

Two weeks later, they awoke to Marta and her children gone from the house. Ludovico, called Quinto, had left a letter announcing their elopement. It was as if in that moment, the moment of reading the letter, someone had inserted an axe into the crack made by his mother's death, and twisted until the whole thing split. All at once the fellowship they'd founded was no longer sacred, their group ceased to exist as a unit of meaning. My painter went back to Turin, and never returned to the villa.

In Turin, it was as if he realized how much time he had to make up for, he began writing for a friend's paper, a communist publication, anti-fascist. His swerve from art to politics was total, once he'd raised his head above the water and inhaled he could no longer return. He didn't paint at all for the next three years, nothing, not so much as an editorial cartoon. It was 1932, there was work to be done.

The pasta arrived and we arranged plates. There was so much I didn't know about the years she was describing, fascists, Mussolini, the self-proclaimed duce, sure, but none of the details, it had always been enough for me to see where it ended, the privilege of all Americans born after the war. He did go back to painting, Anna continued, during his exile. He was arrested for his anti-government writing in 1935, imprisoned in Milan for three months before they sent him to the south. Can you imagine the sun on those white clay hills when you haven't seen daylight for twelve weeks? It was a common thing then, to reduce the prison sentence to exile, they figured the prisoners couldn't do any harm. You've read the memoir, yes? The mail was brought in once a day by an old woman on a donkey, all of it was read and censored by the fascist official of the town, all of the letters sent and received there. No one visited the town, there was no reason for anyone to go there, he was completely cut off. He made no attempt to contact his comrades or resume his political activities, he completely abandoned his previous work. So what did he have to do but to paint, to return to his art. His paintings changed there, you know, have you seen them? I said, apologetically, that I wasn't sure, I'd only seen images of his work online, but the paintings often weren't dated. Some of them are in Rome, she said, almost sternly, naming a villa that had been turned into a museum. You must go and see them.

She smiled forgivingly as our plates were cleared. Can you imagine, by the time he got to the village, he was only thirty-seven, he'd already had three lives. What was he to do? He walked the village, he observed its colors and inhabitants, he painted them. He found himself in a white-dust-covered world where the majority of people thought themselves at the level of wild animals, unuseful to humankind. So he painted the peasants, he never painted any of the town gentry, though it's clear from his letters this created resentments and probably made his time there more unpleasant. But this was his gift to them, the peasants, painting their faces, affirming they were also human beings.

I asked her to tell me about how he died, what happened to him after his release from the village. I still hadn't finished the biography, the arrest and legalese of his sentencing had mired me in a particularly difficult chapter, since I'd known I was soon to meet Anna I'd been unmotivated to push through. She nodded and refilled my glass from the bottle of sparkling water, then looked me squarely in the eye. He wrote the memoir of the village in the years after his release, in his childhood home in Turin. It's incredible, she continued, for each place he lived in his adult life he had a different mode of expression. By the time he died, I sometimes wonder if he thought that he'd already run through all of his possibilities. I wonder if he wanted to start over yet again. His older sister encouraged him to write the book, do you know about his sister? She was the great relationship of his life, I think. Their letters to each other are full of such tenderness, I felt bad for reading them during my research.

It was his sister and her husband who decided they needed to leave Italy. She'd married a man from a similar family from Turin, Jewish, she and her husband were both doctors. Their father, already old when he and his sister were born, was frail, and her two children were still quite small. But her husband had his ear to the ground, the deportations had started farther south. They went to a town called Agno, on the Swiss border, where people in normal times vacationed on a huge glacial lake, and joined a camp of other refugees. There had already been a flood of people crossing the border, but most had been trying to get to France, the Swiss had been tolerant about them passing through. But now France was in the hand of the Germans, people were crossing the border to stay in Switzerland, and the attitude of the Swiss government had changed. They said they were afraid of their high rate of unemployment. The information was fluctuating day by day, a few weeks before they were letting in only military refugees and uniforms of various armies were scattered through the camp, now they were letting in only the politically persecuted, not the racially targeted. The painter might have had a chance to qualify, as a communist, but he refused to leave his family. Sometimes the Swiss let a few people in and stopped at the seventh person, sometimes they required papers that did not exist, sometimes the Italian carabinieri shot those who had hired fishermen to smuggle them across the lake if they were intercepted before they reached the opposite shore. The family was there for weeks, growing increasingly desperate, they didn't think they'd ever be let across.

Anna signaled to the waiter, who brought us two espressos a few minutes later. He took morphine tablets from his sister's medical supplies, she continued, and wandered into a small stable on the outskirts of the town. It was October, it would have been cold in the mountains, it must have seemed a warm place. The next morning the officials changed their minds, they were to be let across, the whole family, everyone was ecstatic, but no one could find him. When they did they had to leave the body behind, they paid some villagers to dig a quick grave, on a hill near the churchyard. And then they went into Switzerland. No one knows where the grave is, or on what hill, his sister always claimed to have no memory of that day, with its violent elations and upsets, and his father died in Geneva four months after they arrived. His sister was the one who found the memoir among his things, she was the one to get it published after the war. With the papers, they also found a note asking to be buried in Aliano. She gave me a small smile as I exhaled, trying to slow my heartbeat, which always seemed to speed up in response to sadness it could do nothing about.

I left money on top of the bill for the waiter to clear with our glasses, and as we moved to gather our things I asked Anna what had interested her in the painter, how she'd first been drawn into her research. She replied that in her first degree she'd been focused on the restoration of paintings, she thought she would work for a museum of a historical trust. It was only for her dottorato that she began to focus on this group, on the other side of the art. She hadn't really considered the painter's memoir, she said. In Italy we read it mostly for its descriptions of southern poverty, but his paintings are so affecting, and he wrote plenty else, brilliant things, and now the only people who read them are people like me, who only come across them after five years of university study. He was capable of great volumes of work, his output of paintings, his journalistic writings, the memoir. I think he was a person who never knew quite what to do with the freedoms he'd been given, but the thing that drew me to his art, to his writing, the thing I couldn't get out of my mind, is that this group existed for five years, maybe less? They were trying to find a different way, apart from politics, through art. These people cared so much about ideas, beauty, they gave everything in their lives to these questions, they didn't care about their families or mistresses, not really, just art and their discussions of it, and they lived this way so purely for half a decade, they built their whole adult lives on it, only to watch the earth upon which they thought they lived crumble beneath them so that they were left with dust in their hands. None of it mattered, in the end they were all swept away in one way or another by the regime, by the war, and the whole world they lived for ceased to exist almost overnight. All of the things they cared about turned out to be totally irrelevant in the face of this violence, this absolutism. Of course it mattered, we still talk about their art, their ideas, but in most ways, now I think that in the most important ways, it didn't matter at all.

After she received her dottorato, Anna continued as we walked down the busy street with its graffitied short buildings, greens glimpsed through the fences suggesting gardens beyond, she'd been given a research fellowship and had spent three months in Germany, in Frankfurt. She'd met another student on the same fellowship while there, a Norwegian. They both found the city soulless and chilly, though he studied economics and, she said, was more predisposed to the atmosphere of black suits and tall gray architecture. They would walk along the river together in the endless rain, would buy ten-euro train tickets to small towns along the Rhine, would spend their nights together in their cramped temporary residences. I fell in love with him, she said, pausing on the ball of her foot and turning to meet my eyes, as if tempting me to challenge her. I met her gaze, and we continued walking. But the relationship quickly took on an edge of antagonism, she said, at least on my part. I'd never been jealous before, never particularly interested even in physical affection, in fact the men I'd known or considered dating during my studies in Rome and before that in Pisa had annoyed me with their attentions, with their physicality, their need. Kristian was the opposite, it was hard to justify my jealousy because he never seemed to flirt with anyone, but he never seemed to betray any feeling toward me either. He would tell me things, in a matter-of-fact tone, like he wanted us to live together in Norway or in Italy, that he loved me, even, he did say it a few times, and I would repeat the things he had said back to myself later and try to inject feeling into them. But I was never able to feel from him that he felt anything, never felt that these feelings existed outside of words, and it began to drive me crazy. I would pick fights that I knew were insane, I would do it in public, I would flirt with his friends in front of him, I even slapped him once, but nothing I did, nothing I ever did, would get an emotional reaction from him. I'm embarrassed of how I behaved, especially since there were other students on the fellowship who witnessed many of these things, I tried to stop, my actions seemed insane to me when I wasn't with him, I tried to be concerned for my professional reputation, but I couldn't, it all seemed worth it to me when he was there, the chance to get any sort of rise out of him, to make him veer even slightly off the path of whatever he was already going to do. Eventually it came to a breaking point, I felt as if I'd been throwing my body against a brick wall for weeks, and we split up and I returned to Italy. And I still can't figure out what it was, if it was love that caused me to behave this way, or if it was something else, something within me reacting to him like a chemical that can't tolerate others of a similar atomic nature.

Chapter Ten

Most of the painter's works, I learned from outdated tourist websites, were in a small museum in Aliano, or at the university in Turin with his archives. A handful were in Liguria, near his family's home there, but a dozen or so were in Rome, as Anna had mentioned, and after our dinner I felt the need to see them as soon as I could. Vietri had been less in my thoughts since I'd started learning about the painter, his story had eclipsed the others in my mind, and I needed it come full circle, to see if it would merge with Vietri's. When I brought up the museum's website to check the hours of admission, I saw that the villa, located off the flank of the Sapienza, was the one in which the self-called duce had lived during his years in Rome. The small collection of twentieth-century art was an afterthought, it seemed most visitors went to tour his bomb shelter. I found these coincidences of Italian history completely ridiculous. There was no room in Italy, everything had happened in the same places, so the painter's work hung in the home of the very fascist leader whose regime had arrested and exiled him, a home built, I read, on top of thirteen thousand square meters of Jewish catacombs, occupied by the very person who would murder his country's Jews. What was one to do with all of this? Nothing could ever be only one thing in Rome, everything had already been touched by so many wars, traumas, millennia, the city was greedy for history, what other city laid claim simultaneously to two separate myths of its own foundation? I'd been reading a book on ancient Rome from Loredana's husband's collection, it had already been two thousand years since Juvenal lamented how a crowded settlement had been allowed to be built on the site of a holy spring where a water spirit had once seduced the second king of Rome. It was as if the Confederacy had surrendered on the same rock where Manhattan had been purchased for beads and silver spoons, if Andy Warhol's factory had discovered Incan mummies interred in the building's foundations, it would never happen, in America we had too much space, and we had the bliss of leaving our physical spaces free of their histories, only in the last four hundred of ten thousand years of occupation of the continent had this level of minutia been recorded for the subsequent generations. It was no wonder the members of my family felt no true sense of individuality outside of the group, and I shuddered, imagining the sticky ties that were already trying to pull me in, and down, away from my pure and unentangled self. Nothing was ever able to stand for just itself in Rome.

I decided to ask Loredana if she'd like to accompany me to see the paintings, I had a desire to see her outside of the apartment, I wanted to shake her out of her calcified grief. I'd finally googled to find the name of Loredana's husband on a website commemorating the Italian victims of terrorism during the years 1969 to 2003. He'd been on an advisory council to the finance ministry, the killing had been claimed by the Red

Brigades. Eventually, a pair of twenty-seven-year-olds had been sentenced, they would have been released from prison around the time Benedetta died. What did one do, I wondered about Loredana, when one's losses tracked one's country's so closely?

We arrived in a taxi and climbed the dozen wide steps at the front of the villa slowly, carefully, Loredana lifting one foot and then another with such effort I wished I could carry her in my arms. But I hadn't remembered, hadn't known, hadn't thought to look up, that there was no elevator inside the building, and the paintings were on the third floor, the Italian third floor at that. She wasn't able to climb that many stairs. She was unfazed and patted my arm. Go see your paintings. I can wait in the garden. I protested, it felt rude to leave her. We compromised that we would tour the ground floor with its grand furnishings together, and then she would wait for me in the garden on the grounds. We wandered the ornate, jewel-colored rooms, the ballroom Pepto-Bismol pink and smaller than I might have thought, the erstwhile duce had used it to house his billiards table. Loredana had told me she had never visited before, but she remained impassive in the face of this luxurious history. I thought of asking if she had any memories of these years, but the history was so deep, there were so many layers the question might disturb that they exerted their own force of inertia. The Italians I knew rarely talked about this part of their historical past, or else it was so coded I had yet to observe that they did.

I descended the front stairs with Loredana, who moved her foot laboriously down each step as if there were a foreign object attached to each leg. The day was perfect, dry and sunny, the kind I imagined monasteries awaited to make paper or harvest hops. I walked her to a bench on the grounds, surrounded by purple flowers, and she waved me off. I reentered the villa and climbed the stairs quickly, as if there were a creature set to attack my heels. The rooms on the first-second floor were all painted with themes chosen in the seventeenth century, as there were no hallways I spiraled upwards through them, one covered in hieroglyphics, another with the feats of Alexander the Great, my sense of reality was becoming unmoored by my surroundings, looking at the trompe l'oeil on the ceiling of the bedroom of the duce himself I imagined the large body looking up at a clever painting designed to trick him into thinking he could see to infinity. I realized I disliked picturing evil, powerful men naked, and left the room quickly. As I did I felt a chill, and noticed that I had been alone in these rooms. The tourists were gone, the summer had passed.

The next room I entered was full of scenes depicting the myth of Cupid and Psyche, the god still asleep with Psyche's disloyal lamp above him, Psyche prostrate before Venus, then the mighty Jupiter. It was the myth I'd found the most romantic as a teenager, married to a spouse she'd never seen, visited only at night, unsure even if her husband was a human being, learning, in the end, he wasn't. It only occurred to me now that this myth was about penance.

The top floor of the villa housed the small collection of twentieth-century art. These rooms had none of the ornate detailing of the previous three levels, rather, the beige walls seemed thin and temporary. I went straight to the room with the painter's works, suddenly impatient, and I stood in the center for a few minutes, looking at none of them closely, instead letting the colors and landscapes absorb into my peripheral vision, trying to transport myself. There was a sole self-portrait and I went closer, in it I could see that the painter would have been a good-natured old man, rotund, with something vulnerable in his soft large brown eyes, cow-like, searching for approval and accepting of the world's flaws. I wondered at the early years of his life in Turin as the city awoke, mechanical, enlarging itself with haphazard parts. He had the long gentle fingers of an artist, not meant for industrial labor, let alone armed struggle.

The paintings done in Liguria in the years he'd lived in the villa were all rich purples and blues, the lines were primitive and worried over like those in cave paintings, as if the details of the persons were yet to be filled in. It was the paintings he did in the village that moved me, Anna was right, there was a change, the greens were so deep they were almost black, the lines were thicker, the paint more decisive on the canvas. The landscapes of the town and the surrounding hills were the color of sun-bleached bone, while the people were in pinks and sallow greens, faces and forms repeating through the dozen half canvases, the eyes of the peasants wary and resigned. The scenes depicted were desolate, provincial, hills and animals and dust and sunsets like dried blood. No water in sight, the occasional single tree. But there was a yearning conveyed by the scenes, I felt the pull.

One painting in particular drew me in, it was of a boy, his eyebrows long and thin, his nose aquiline, his expression cocky and calm, both searching and all-knowing, a goat slung confidently around his shoulders like the stole of a wealthy woman. The caption titled it *La Squadrista*, and I wondered at the name, I couldn't remember any fascist squads or Blackshirts present in the memoir. He looked too young, fourteen or maybe fifteen, and his eyes had no violence. He appeared in several of the paintings, I noticed, in two he was among a group of boys, and I thought I could make him out in a large canvas depicting several families of the town. I looked into his face. Given the date of the paintings, he would have been the same age as Vietri.

I found it difficult to sleep that night, my thoughts turned over and over, kept returning to the boy in the painting from Aliano, la squadrista, and his long clever eyes. I was curious, I could have waited until morning and reread the book, waiting to see if he was mentioned, but I was impatient and sleepless and I discovered that some kind soul had uploaded the copyright-expired English translation onto the internet. I opened a search bar in the window of the text of the memoir and quietly typed in the words. "La squadrista," the nickname had been kept in Italian, appeared six times. Given perhaps a page and a half of the book, he is first mentioned as one of the boys who roam the village throughout the day, who treat the painter as a welcome curiosity, an emissary from a world with nothing in common with their own. School had been a vague presence in their lives, already in the past. Sometimes the younger boys search out the painter and find him in the graveyard, where he naps in open, unassigned holes, the only place of shade to be found in the deforested landscape. They are not from the peasant families, their parents have spent their lives in petty competition for the few government jobs. The older boys, the ones who would have gone to America a few years before, are now trapped by the immigration quota, they have nowhere to go. La squadrista is fifteen and desperate to get out of the village, he speaks to the painter about his plans to enlist in the war in Ethiopia without using the words enlist, army, war, or Ethiopia. Go to Africa, he says instead. I must go to Africa. He has five years until he can join the army, and he is despondent at the thought that he might miss the war.

It was clear to me reading these pages that the painter meant this nickname ironically, even slightly affectionately, and that the boy, la squadrista, has no idea of the connotations the word had acquired in the world outside the village. Milan, the north, factories, snow, fascist squads, these things are as far away to him as Africa. He is already nominally a party member, as all the boys were compelled to be, his name had been sent to the office of the military district in the year of his birth. He repeats to the painter, matter-of-factly, I must get out, it's my only card. Why not go to Africa?

It was still night when I finished rereading these excerpts, and I was quiet as I moved through the apartment to my room. I was intrigued by the squadrista's story, moreover in my long hours of consideration of the bureaucratic traces of Vietri's existence that might be available to me, it hadn't occurred to me to look up military records. Vietri was born in 1920, he would have been eligible to enlist in 1940, by the time that war in Ethiopia had shifted and grown, like a monster devouring other monsters, had become the Second World War. I only vaguely knew anything about this history. There'd been fighting in Africa, with the British, I thought.

I'd never heard anyone on my Italian side of the family talk about the war, I knew my mother's father had been too young for the army, and I'd never thought to ask. California was so different, my father's father had been in the navy, had fought in the Pacific, I'd grown up knowing that history, had written school reports on his elopement with my grandmother while on leave. Of course the war was romantic and noble to Americans, but in Northern California it was closer to a foundational myth, the industries that employed my friends' parents, Lockheed, Boeing, the port, all sprung from that conflict. Even the shame we carried, the internment of Japanese families, was not ignored, many of those now empty dusty enclosures weren't far from Sacramento, but it was so cleanly handled by our textbooks as to be dismissive, the one moral mistake we'd made, and look how we were owning up to it, with this month of fifth-grade history. But how could it be that way for Italy, which had been both occupier, then occupied? They'd colonized Ethiopia, Somalia, Libya, invaded Slovakia, Albania, Greece, but had then been invaded themselves by the Germans, their country split into two with civil wars enacted in both halves, even before the final invasion by a motley group of British, American, and occasionally Polish armies. It was bewildering to imagine, even these decades later, the history was so complicated it confused empathy.

It had never occurred to me to ask Andrea about his military service, he'd been born in the cutoff year, the last one in which it was mandatory in Italy, though I'd always assumed he'd avoided it by enrolling in university. If I'd been a boy, born a few months after him in the new year, I would have been of the first generation free. The draft was such an antiquated word to me, in Berkeley it was spoken of as I imagined very superstitious medieval populations spoke of dragons. I couldn't picture Andrea holding a gun, in one of those funny hats. Andrea who was always so calm, so in control, I couldn't see this Andrea taking orders, folding precise bedsheets, I had only the vaguest notions of what being a soldier entailed in the modern world. Andrea could be imperious, but he was gentle.

I tried to square my preferred image of Vietri, elderly, in dusty book-reflected light, with one of him young, as a soldier. My imagination failed. But what did I know of boys, really? I'd known a lot of them, plenty in the biblical sense, but I'd grown up without brothers, a distinction I'd always found essential. The boys I'd dated, the ones I'd known in my travels, all of them had been nice. But how then to explain the terrible things that had happened, over and over, often on the very ground of this city? Its own namesake had murdered his twin. Earlier that week I had come across a casual reference in my book, or at least it seemed casual to me, for how could it ever be written with enough gravity, I'd forced myself to read the Italian sentence several times to make sure the verbs were what I thought they were, to the fact that the emperor Nero had kicked to death his pregnant wife. I found my hand on my stomach at the memory. I thought of the final sentence of the *Aeneid*, in which Rome is born as Aeneas kills the wounded Turnus, Turnus who pleads, from the ground, "Go no further down the road of hatred," Aeneas who implants his sword to the hilt in the prostrate man's breast anyway, this planting of the sword simultaneous with his founding of the city, the same Latin verb. That is to say, it did occur to me as I filled out this next request form I'd found online, as I put Chiara Vietri under the name of the requestor, as I filled in granddaughter under relation, as I wrote in my own name and Loredana's address on the return envelope, as I put it in the mail, it did occur to me that looking up Vietri's military records could lead me to something I wasn't sure I wanted to know. Someone had to commit war crimes. Not all boys could be good.

Chapter Eleven

I'd gotten into the habit of a long morning walk across the city to acquire a certain pastry once or twice a week. My route took me across the river as it sloped south to what I thought of as the Vatican side, through wide avenues shaded by enormous trees. I liked this part of the city, liked the surprise of a small triangular concrete island at an intersection with nothing but a bench and a trash can around which a whole block could orient itself. On one of these outings, perhaps three weeks after I'd requested the military records, my cell phone rang just as I passed one of these anchors, and I winced, I knew my Pronto? would give me away to the teenage boys leaning against walls observing it all from a remove of two hundred feet, I'd never been able to get the roll going on the *r*. Distracted by these self-conscious thoughts, I answered the phone to the sharp, patient voice of my aunt Giulia.

I asked how she'd gotten my number and felt immediately ashamed, I hadn't intended for it to be the first thing out of my mouth, but Giulia was unfazed, as, I remembered, she always was. Your father, she said. I'd given my father the number in case of emergency, it seemed the daughterly thing to do, the small offering I could make, but I hadn't known that he was in touch with any of my aunts, it had never occurred to me that the channels of communication did not flow solely through myself. The street had become still, strange. I asked how often she and my father spoke, and she said every month or two. I felt my world lifting and realigning, the ground shifting under me. I'd assumed when I'd stopped my summers in Rome, when I'd been absent from my grandfather's funeral, I'd assumed that these ties had been permanently loosened, that I had changed something that I would have difficulty getting back. Giulia's voice interrupted, I'll be in town soon. I'd like to hear about your travels.

We agreed to meet for lunch in a few days, and I hung up the phone bewildered, my shoulders jerking strangely, tallying the assumptions about my own life that had just been called into question. I fiddled with my phone as I walked, pushing in the buttons though I knew the screen was locked. It calmed me, my hand and the phone both hidden in the pocket of my jacket, walking up the stone steps to the bridge, blind to those around me. Who could I call? I'd been so deeply alone with my thoughts these last months, the conversations I'd had with other travelers tended to be utterly mundane or cosmically deep, there was none of the usual airing of thoughts that I'd found had come with living with my boyfriend, though by the end there was so much I'd been keeping to myself that it had in fact been much longer since I'd had this release. The phone twirled in my fingers. Call Andrea? Settimia? Loredana? I had no desire to talk to my father, and it was not out of betrayal, but I felt our relationship had shifted fundamentally, and I wanted more time to feel the contours of this change. He'd always wanted me to connect with my mother's side, it was why I'd been sent to Rome for those summers in the first place. He was an only child, the only one of his family on the West Coast, I know he believed it was my only chance to grow up with a family.

My aunts had found out about the departure of my grandfather a few years after I'd stopped my Roman summers, one Sunday when their keys no longer worked in the locks of the apartment they'd grown up in, had visited every week, the apartment they'd expected to inherit, the apartment soon to be owned and occupied by an American professor of art history and his third wife. The drama reached me secondhand, conveyed by Giulia over the phone. But I'd felt unaffected, the impact of the betrayal wasn't capable of sustaining itself across an ocean and another continent. What did the dark apartment where I'd spent some chaotic and vaguely unhappy summers have to do with me, with my college applications and summer job as a lifeguard, driving aimlessly through the valley with my friends on the weekends, with chilly nights spent drinking cheap vodka with juice in empty orchards. When he'd died, less than a year later, I had just started college. The coffin had arrived from France, sent by, as my aunts put it, his Algerian whore. The funeral took place during my first week of classes at Berkeley, and it was one of the few times my father had involved himself in my relationship with my aunts. My mother, to our surprise, had agreed with her doctors that it wasn't a good idea for her to attend, they thought it was too triggering based on previous delusions, and by the time my father told me the date of the funeral he'd already informed my aunts neither I nor my mother would be coming. Your education is more important, he said. I felt relieved, that this decision had been taken away from me, but I also wondered what I would have done, what I would have chosen. The next time I saw my mother I told her I was sorry for her loss, and she gave me a sharp startled glance I wasn't able to interpret.

I had so few distinct memories of my grandfather. I remembered him in corners, reading, or doing a sudoku, a recent hobby, seated in an armchair, never at the center. Once he told me, just as I was exiting the apartment with my cousins, that my top was cut too low, and I burned with shame around him for the rest of the summer. He'd said the same thing to all of my female cousins at one point or another, they assured me, but only I seemed to take it seriously. I'd put the top, of which I'd formerly been so proud, it was from Urban Outfitters, which felt like the epitome of grown-up fashion to me at the age of thirteen, back into my suitcase and didn't wear it again for the rest of the summer.

The drama with the nurse that caused so much pain to my aunts and their children was for me a backdrop in the blurred dark space of my teenage years. My grandfather hadn't needed a physical aide, during the summers I had seen him, but his memory was failing. Who are you? he would ask, and I would tell him I was my mother's daughter, and he would rub my shoulder and say, that's good. Sometimes he would ask where she was, and I would say California, and he would shake his head indulgently and correct me, that's too far, she would never go so far. On other days he would tell me where she was, she just went to buy some olives, assuring me she'd be back soon. Or he would say, she's in the kitchen with her sisters, can't you hear them? Often, he would slip into the dialect of his village near Salerno, and I would wave over Andrea or Giulia, helpless to understand. I was grateful that he never mistook me for my mother, he often called my female cousins by their mothers' names, the time he lived in was fluid, I existed in the present, and my cousins were emissaries from thirty years before, though this never seemed to confuse him, or even to offer any contradiction. So that, in his reality, some of his daughters and their generation had teenage children, while some were children themselves, and there was a peace with which he accepted all of these facts. The only thing that caused me grief, because it upset my aunts, was his inability to acknowledge the previous existence of my grandmother. Unlike what he thought about my mother, he was never convinced my grandmother was at the store or in the next room. He simply never mentioned her, and if one of my aunts sat down next to him and tried to introduce a memory, he would ask, abruptly, who's Claudia? Who's Mamma? And if they tried to tell him, then he would say, I've never been married, I'm too young. Maybe one day I'll find a girl. But I saw that my aunts did this less and less as time went on, that it was too painful to lose their mother, over and over, every time their father denied her existence. I wondered, now, if that was why they got the nurse in the first place. No one in the family could have kept him at home? They were busy, yes, Giulia had always traveled for work and Settimia's mother-in-law lived with her and her husband, Giacomo, but

I thought I understood how living with someone who would deny your best memories, the ones you kept closest since there wouldn't be any more to come, would be too hard, day after day. They would have had to choose, his reality or theirs. And I suppose in this way they both chose their mother.

I was still in the street, walking toward somewhere I no longer remembered, but my fingers were texting Andrea. Come, he replied, there's someone I want you to meet. I walked there, he was with some friends at a café, and I recognized his imperious posture as I approached, his ridiculous acid-wash jeans low on his hips, his arm slung around a figure almost his height, whose hair-darkened chin tilted up to Andrea's ear to say something I couldn't yet hear, and I saw Andrea smile, and then I saw everything I hadn't been seeing since I'd arrived in Rome, and when Andrea had introduced me to the boy, his ragazzo, Fahad, an engineering student, born in Lahore, it felt as if all that had been floating since I'd answered Giulia's call had fallen back to earth, had assumed new form, one that was more solid, a landscape in which I could learn to navigate.

I went with Andrea and Fahad back to Fahad's dorm kitchen at the university, a white cavernous space with cheap appliances where he cooked us an extremely competent risotto while other foreign students wandered occasionally in and out. I teased Andrea, who of course couldn't even boil water. I had to explain to them the expression. Fahad had the shaggy haircut of a '90s movie star, his eyelids tended downwards toward a sleepy droop. Their physical comfort with each other was evident, their touches were casual, but they would lean unexpectedly on each other as if each was the other's favorite tree. I smiled broadly at them over my risotto, but inwardly I mourned the time I had wasted by not seeing. What other facts about my family had I failed to notice? At what cost had my search for Vietri come?

Lunch with Giulia was pleasant. We met in Monti, in the heart of the city, at a restaurant she deemed good at the classics. She'd always tried to impose on me a loyalty to Roman cooking, shrugging as she ordered for us, Thursday gnocchi, Saturday tripe, a horrific phrase I'd forgotten. Fortunately it was Thursday. She'd traveled widely, to several of the places I had been in the last year, and we talked of Bolivia, the south of Argentina. I'd always been slightly afraid of her sharp humor, I suppose in my teenage years it had reminded me of my mother's cutting remarks, but over lunch I found a witty warmth that was easy to fall into and enjoy. I wondered if she had always been this way, the idea of adults having distinguishable personalities was only just becoming available to me at fifteen, and I didn't trust my previous observations. I asked her, tentatively, how long Andrea had been out to the family, and she told me seven years. But his mother has always known. I thought of Settimia, and suddenly felt that if I were to speak I would cry. So I let Giulia talk of the nonprofit she worked for in London, the work they did in Africa, her partner, a Hungarian who worked for the British Museum. She told me of the rest of the family: Dida had been living in Paris, had just had a baby, was about to move back to Rome. Clea had a law degree, Andrea was still working to complete his dottorato, which seemed to be a source of humor I didn't quite understand. When she asked, toward the end of the meal, why I hadn't told her I was in Rome, I shrugged and said I hadn't been sure if I was ready to stay. She squeezed my hand and told me she understood. I realized that Giulia had left, too.

As we exited the restaurant, we walked naturally next to each other, neither of us asking the other if we had anywhere to go. It made it easier to hear the question I knew was coming.

And now?

I wasn't sure.

Would I see the rest of the family?

I didn't know yet. Yes, maybe soon.

Will you stay in Rome?

I didn't know. I wasn't sure.

It felt suddenly silly to me, after we parted and I walked back northwards, climbing toward Parioli, that I had avoided my family for so long, I felt ashamed. It had felt so oppressive when I was younger, these women above me who wanted to guide me and help me and in return know every single thing about my life. I was an only child, my parents were so distant, each in their own way, this board of elders was frightening when they were suddenly thrust in to my life at the age of eleven. Then of course there were also the questions they might have asked about my mother, the memories of her I'd be obliged to dredge up, she was their sister, they would want to know, their loyalty would be to her. They would ask how recently I had seen her, they who had not been able to see her, while for me it was a choice to spend my last months away from her, my failures as a daughter would be exposed. And I was so afraid of being like her, of learning about a childhood similarity between us, something that might indicate I was also destined for her fate. It didn't make sense outside of the fuzzy underside of my brain where the thought lived, but avoiding my family was a way of avoiding the diagnosis, if it were to come.

I'd wanted to make my own way, desperately, but now I saw how tempting it might be, how tempting it was, to sink into these embraces, to absorb these advices, to let myself be connected to this other generation, to take inside myself their lessons and also their fears for me. I had thought this would mean giving up a part of myself, my autonomy, which I'd held so close for so long. But now, was it Italy, was it Rome, was it my failing search for Vietri? I wondered if these ties, these other stories and other lives, might make me better prepared to face my own. After Giulia had kissed both cheeks and told me how glad she was she'd seen me, after I'd caught her arms to give her a hug far too American, close and desperate, I said to her ear, unable to look at her face, that I would like to see Settimia.

The next afternoon, I called my father. He seemed surprised to hear from me when he picked up the phone, it hadn't been long since I'd called on his birthday. I'd thought I might tell him that I'd seen Giulia, to ask about their relationship over the years. But I hesitated, I wasn't yet ready to face the responsibility that would come with this knowledge, so instead I asked him to tell me about Italy in Africa during World War II. Loredana was out, Agnieszka was accompanying her to some appointment, and I was using a phone card on the apartment phone, grateful she wouldn't overhear. My request was based in a habit my father and I had developed as he drove me to high school in the two years before I'd gotten my license. Tell me about this, I would say: black holes, the colonial history of Hong Kong, Supreme Court disputes, there was nothing he couldn't give me a twenty-minute introductory lecture on. I hadn't appreciated it at the time, how can you know about *everything*, I'd ask when I was young. The other fathers I knew were into the Sacramento Kings and their shotguns, or almond farming, the Civil War. You can't be interested in everything, I remembered pleading. My brain has a lot of space, he would say, unbothered, whereas I believed that if I wasn't an expert on something I had no right to an opinion.

So tell me about Africa, I said.

Well, the Italians had already been in Africa a long time before World War II, he said. At the end of the nineteenth century various pacts had given them part of Somalia. They'd invaded Libya in 1910 and set up a colony, and in 1935 the British had let them through the Suez Canal to invade Ethiopia. Ethiopia had been a sovereign kingdom, there had been an outcry in response, but the League of Nations was toothless, they couldn't do anything. By the end of the '30s they had a pact with Germany, so when the Germans invaded France, Italy declared war on France and England as well. Most of the Italian soldiers were already in Africa, and they decided to invade British-held Egypt from Libya. But the British had Malta, they had planes and the Italians had boats, and the British had no trouble sinking the supply ships with their air force. And after Germany invaded Russia, the Italians had no access to oil, they had hardly enough fuel to get the boats they did send across. There were hundreds of thousands of Italian troops in the desert with no water. The Germans had to step in, start escorting the supply ships by air, they sent over Rommel. So then the Germans and the Italians were fighting the British together in North Africa, from Tunisia across to Egypt, with the Germans really in charge. It was all over by 1942. After a major battle over two hundred thousand Italians surrendered all at once and were dispersed into POW camps in the British Empire.

I asked the question I really wanted to know. Well, he said in response, the Italians weren't known for war crimes, like ones that took place elsewhere, it was a gentlemen's war compared to what happened on the Eastern Front.

Chapter Twelve

Vietri's military records were awaiting me when I returned home one day from a long walk, Loredana had placed the large envelope of thick dark paper on my pillow. I opened it and slid out a single sheet. I read it quickly, wondering if I would need Andrea's help to understand it, but the information was so sparse that I'd finished my own translation within fifteen minutes despite the antiquated lettering of the handwriting and the low quality of the photocopy. Here were Vietri's age, place of birth, height, eye color, and the date of his enlistment, his parents' names: Pietro and Maddalena. I tried to envision the scant physical picture these few words presented, brown hair, brown eyes, 165 centimeters. My height, five foot five. The image was vague, but I held it in my mind for a few moments triumphantly. But this faded. All it told me, really, was that Vietri had indeed been enlisted in the army. Not where he had gone, what he had done, what type of person he was, where he might be now. I let myself melt onto the bed, an act I rarely permitted myself, my days were so unstructured if I admitted midday naps I was unsure where the sloth would end. But surely, I thought, this couldn't be the only record of his military service. I turned over and reexamined the paper. What I'd received was called a lista d'estrazione, but I remembered there'd been several options when I'd requested it, other words I didn't know. Had I selected the wrong one?

I rolled myself off the bed, resigned to return to Google, but as I walked softly past the living room, I saw Loredana in an armchair, reading. I hesitated, it occurred to me that I could ask her. She looked up. The idiom between Loredana and myself still had not yet been firmly established, and I tended to present all sentences formally as if opening a topic for debate. Is it true that your husband was in the army? I asked. She took off her glasses, shifting slightly in her chair. It was after the war, she said. This was in the '50s. It's how we met, actually. She gestured to a spot near her on the sofa. I'll tell you the story some other time. Now, why do you want to know about military records? My breath caught, and for a moment my thoughts spun outward, wondering how she had known, what other secrets she'd cracked open. Then I calmed. The return sender on the envelope had been from the archive of the military district.

There's a man, I began, attempting to become one with my spot of couch, a man who I used to communicate with in Berkeley, when I worked for a bookstore there. He used to order hundreds of books, but he was in Rome. When I came here, I thought I'd look him up, but I couldn't find him. He's very old. So now, I spread my hands open in my lap, it's not really for any reason, but I'd like to know about him. I'd like to know if he's alive, I'd like to meet him, but if I can't, I'd also like to know about his life. I, well, I thought the military records might be a way to find out more about what happened to him even if I couldn't find him. I trailed off, my eyes drawn out the window. I felt unburdened, deeply shaken, exposed, suddenly overwhelmed by a childish desire to run to my room and bury myself in blankets. Loredana reached out and gave a comforting squeeze to my arm.

Loredana withdrew her hand, took a quiet sip of her tea, and I looked away, blinking. There are several forms, she said. The lista d'estrazione can tell you if he was drafted. But there's something called the foglio matricolare, it will tell you more of what happened, places, promotions, things like that. She studied my face. I can ask my lawyer to request this for you, she said, would that be helpful? The bureaucracy can be complicated, usually the request needs to come from a relative, these things move faster if the request is from a lawyer. I pay him either way, she said. Every month, for anything that comes up. With the way my husband died, some things with Benedetta . . . there were lots of complications. I gave her a questioning look, and she sighed. In the years before she died, Benedetta had some problems with drugs. It was a boyfriend who got her into it, she never stole from me. I gave her a small smile, and then took a breath slowly, looking around the room with its rich colors and complicated lines, wondering if I was becoming a person who could accept help. Yes, I said finally. I would love that.

Giulia texted the next day to ask if I wanted to visit Nero's palace, the Domus Aurea, with her and Settimia, I must have mentioned my reading on the Roman emperors during our lunch. It had been closed to the public for years for repairs after the walls had partly collapsed after a rainstorm, always just about to reopen, but she had a friend, someone her partner knew, who had offered to arrange for us to join one of the semiprivate tours that went on anyway, apparently the chance of the walls failing and crushing us beneath the ruins was only very slight. This was a familiar move, in my previous summers my aunts had always had the habit of analyzing my offhand comments for interests, and it was sweet, I could see now, it had been sweet, but at the time it had felt like they were trying to tie my identity down in a way I resented. I'd looked in horror as my older cousins had to choose tracks in school by the age of sixteen, while I'd desperately wanted to be defined only by my true, inner self, even if I was unsure who, or what, that was.

I stood outside the metal gate above the slope to the Colosseum awaiting my aunts, feeling as if my chest was filled with a thousand buzzing, winged creatures, feeling like I should run away, feeling like if I didn't scream or pull at my hair I might combust. But my mother's frustration had always been directed outward in such ways, I'd long ago learned to direct mine inside. I was surprised by the intensity of my anxiety, but I considered Settimia the emotional heart of my Italian family, now the floodgates would be completely removed. The last time I'd seen her was when she'd driven me to the airport at the end of the summer when I was fifteen, my last summer, and she'd waited with me through the first customs line, a witness as I chose not to use my Italian passport. I now felt ashamed at how flagrantly I'd rejected the idea that I also belonged to this country, but at the time it had felt like a gesture of authenticity. I saw my two aunts crest the hill, Giulia short and energetic, her walk purposeful, marchlike, Settimia seeming to trail her, taller but somehow conveying less of her presence to the world. She moved faster upon seeing me, passed ahead of Giulia, straight to me, straight to my cheeks, which she kissed, and then she hugged me close and welcomed me back to Rome. She looked older than she had the last time I'd seen her, the ten years were there on her face and her hair was a new color, slightly red and garish. Giulia, the oldest of the three sisters, appeared the same, her gray had appeared in her dark hair before I'd met her and had hardly spread in the intervening years, she had performed her aging early and now appeared youthful by comparison.

It was cool and damp underground, and Settimia and I shivered at the same time, absorbing the stream of facts emerging from our guide, a short, energetic man who recalled to me a nineteenth-century church custodian, he had the uncertain social abilities of an archaeologist, the result of a career performed mostly underground, an existence lived between two time periods. He spoke in English, which Giulia must have arranged, and she translated softly to Settimia from time to time following cues I wasn't able to understand. Settimia had not let go of my arm, she pulled me close as I listened, and I was glad to lean into her warmth. The palace had only existed for a handful of years, within a decade of Nero's death the walls had been stripped of their ivory, jewels, and gold inlay, his successor had the palace filled in with dirt and rubble, had built a bathhouse on top of the ruins that the duce, who, two millennia later, wanted to be a Roman emperor himself, replaced with a rose garden that threatened to wash away what was left below with every rainstorm. The palace had been rediscovered in the Renaissance when a young boy fell into what he thought was a cave of painted walls. Artists began to climb down on ropes with candles to look at the figures and called the style of art grotesque, from grotto, cave. It was strange, the paths that words took, for this was also the emperor who was accused of burning half the city to make room for his palace grounds, who killed his mother, two of his wives, his brother, and himself, who was said to dip Christians in oil and set them on fire to light the pathways of gardens in the evenings. At last, he was quoted, upon entering this palace where flower petals rained from a gilded ceiling that rotated during dinner parties, where guests were greeted by a ninety-eight-foot-tall bronze statue of himself, at last, he said, at last I can live like a human being. And then it had become a cave. Grotesque referred first not to these actions but to the patterns on the wall depicting human-animal hybrids, limbs turned into branches, humans into lions, cupids' bottoms into fish tails, and I thought I understood how these creatures could speak to this world. What did it mean to be a human being?

We turned into a room our guide named as the cave room, on the ceiling Odysseus reached out to offer the cyclops the fateful glass of wine. Look how considered this was, our guide was saying, gesturing to the ceiling. His bald head gleamed ee-rily in the dim light. It had been a bathroom, a fountain ran down the side of the wall, and Nero, committing fully to the theme, had instructed the ceiling to be covered in fake stalac-tites. So there were a lot of bad things with this emperor, our guide continued in a ludicrously neutral tone, there were a lot of bad things, he said, but look at this planning, this consider-ation. I wanted to laugh. A Nero apologist.

I'd been absorbed in the tour, my thoughts remained in previous millennia, so when we entered again into the sunlight I was unprepared for Settimia's determined expression. You'll come for lunch now, yes? she asked, and I moved my head slightly and started to say that I was expected at Loredana's, and in truth I was, but mostly I wanted to retreat to my room, retreat from the family, to think about Nero, that archaeol-ogist, why the actions and aesthetic decisions of an emperor dead for two thousand years had been more real to me than the family I'd been standing next to. But I wasn't prepared for Settimia's angry tears, for her to let go of my arm and turn at me sharply, wasn't prepared for the things she shouted at me in Italian in front of the bewildered tourists making their way down the slope of the rose garden to the Colosseum, I wasn't prepared for Giulia to be the one to pull her back, to mutter softly in her tall ear, to give me a sympathetic smile, Giulia who I'd been the most scared of, I wasn't prepared to run from Settimia's anger into the metro, wasn't prepared for the click of the clasp on my purse on the empty stairs, for the twelve-year-old boy to vanish into the crowd on the platform, my cell phone in his hands, so that I wouldn't know if they had tried to follow me, if Settimia had called me to continue to yell or to apologize. Instead I was left alone underground, shaking and empty-handed, my breath strange in my lungs, looking around at my fellow tourists and wondering if they were threats.

Chapter Thirteen

The foglio matricolare arrived from Loredana's lawyer the next week in a heavy, formal envelope, the name of the firm embossed on the outside. The photocopy was dark, the letters obscured at a crease in the middle, but the document had been transcribed into type, with an English translation affixed to the back. I glanced over the original, briefly, before turning to the translation, grateful I hadn't had to again decipher the strange handwriting and abbreviations. The dates spanned from 1940 to 1946, and the names of the places were strange: Ravenna, Tobruk, El Alamein.

I read it all, quickly, standing in the apartment, then again, more slowly, in a too-expensive restaurant near Loredana's apartment. In times of great excitement I was calmed by being alone in public, and I'd ordered a glass of wine, a lemony white, my off-season Jewish artichokes lay on my plate like small dead birds. I usually spent money cheaply, the more expensive something was the more I was reminded of the source of my income, but today I sat alone at my table with my fancy wine as I read and reread the words, shuffling the papers back and forth, trying to cull memories that weren't my own out of nothing more than dates and locations. There was training in the north, in Ravenna, before he'd been sent to Libya, Tobruk, then to El Alamein, the site of a major battle. In February 1941 he was declared a prisoner of war of the English. He was repatriated in 1946, almost a year after the end of the war.

I was bewildered. The facts were in my hands, but instead of detailing a life I could envision, they had made Vietri's story even further from my comprehension. I sipped my wine. His apartment in Rome had yielded nothing, I'd never been to Libya, to England, or even Ravenna, had only vague images from the *Aeneid, Jane Eyre,* sandy beaches and shipwrecks, country manors and exiled children. A life as a list of places and dates, it reminded me of my mother's medical records I'd come across while snooping in my father's papers during high school, the cold, cleanly cut bureaucracy of it was horrifying to me, how could a life be reduced to these few facts? It was a violence I feared for myself, if the diagnosis happened to me, everything I'd thought and felt and feared rendered as a handful of dates, places, medical or military labels, a metamorphosis from human being to data. How did I ever think I would be able to understand Vietri's life, what did the books he had ordered from the store have to do with this list? I wondered what would solve this, meeting Vietri, maybe, or reading a thousand-page novel covering every scene of his life. How would I ever be able to understand the world before me?

I met signora Elena in a leafy piazza in a neighborhood I'd never been to, west of the river. Her aide, Pilar, and I had arranged the meeting over the phone in Spanish. I'd had to get a new cell phone, there was no way to arrange the meeting without one, Romans would have no more gone without a mobile than without shoes. Pilar first had to clear it with signora Elena's two sons, both of whom had migrated north, one to Germany, the other Milan. Fifteen years before, signora Elena's now deceased husband had spoken about his experiences as a prisoner of war in Australia for an oral history project based in London. He'd been in the same unit as Vietri in Libya, had been in Ethiopia before that. Their unit number had been listed in the foglio matricolare, and I'd found her husband's brief account when I'd searched for the number online. I'd then located his widow in the phone directory, at last, the pagine bianche had yielded information, I'd begun to wonder if it was just an aspirational document. I'd known he was from Rome from his testimony and I'd guessed correctly that when he returned he hadn't left again.

When I'd first called, Pilar had told me that if I spoke with signora Elena she wasn't sure what I would get. I didn't know the relevant vocabulary in Spanish, so when I'd asked if she had Alzheimer's or dementia, I'd had to use the English words, and she hadn't understood. I was reduced to asking in Spanish, pathetically, how is her brain? Pilar responded fluidly that it was like a river and you never knew what course it would run through that day, or how muddy the water would be, if it's stormed the day before, of course, she said, it will dredge up the silt, and it will be hard to see through the water, claro? I said it was clear, and I'd wanted to tell her how much I admired how she'd expressed it. But my cheap replacement Nokia seemed like a poor device to convey such a message, and my Spanish had been so wobbled by the recent Italian.

Pilar kissed me on both cheeks when I approached, and I did the same with signora Elena, bending down to her wheelchair, and told her it was a pleasure to meet her. I used the formal address, but my tone was as if I were speaking to a child. It was only when I said her name that she made eye contact with me. I'm named after a queen, you know, she said, gripping my hand as I sat on a bench facing her, she was parked so that only an inch or two remained between us. She must have been ninety, if not older, and her skin felt as cool and smooth as an apple's. I told her I knew that very well, and that I wanted to hear about when she was a girl and Elena was queen and her husband had been in the war. She seemed confused by the noun war, and I clarified, went to Ethiopia, Abyssinia, I corrected, and then again, to Africa. She perked up at the final name. L'AhOoEi, she said, l'aooee. I thought at first she was saying the name of a place I didn't know, but then when I replayed it slowly in my head, I recognized the acronym. L'AOI, Africa Orientale Italiana. I asked if her husband had gone there. She cracked a smile, one that resulted in a bit of drool on the top of her bosom. Pilar wiped it away efficiently. Signora Elena began to sing, quietly, at first, so that I couldn't hear the words . . . Faccetta nera, faccetta nera, she sang. Little black face, she was singing, little black face.

I exchanged glances with Pilar, knew that mine was a panicked expression. The park was full of echoes of her and signora Elena, mostly duos made of an old woman, white hair, white skin, and a young woman with a brown face, or, I supposed, a black one. But no one looked toward us. I drew a breath. Signora Elena, I said, what is that song? Can you tell me about it?

He used to tease me, she said. He'd sing it right here, she raised her hand unsteadily and gestured back toward her earlobe. I made sure we were married when he left, she said with a satisfied straightening of her shoulders.

What did he tell you about the war? I asked. Did you get letters from him?

Oh, yes, yes, she said. Letters from Africa. She slowed her pronunciation: Addis Ababa. She gripped my arm and leaned closer to me. One envelope was full of red sand. No letter, just sand. Like the sun. She occasionally jerked her neck in a strange way that put to mind a deranged bird, an ostrich perhaps, or a turkey, but each word she spat out was clear. I pressed my finger to the grains and put them in my compact. There were not many left after the journey.

What did the other letters say? I asked.

They said what letters say, she replied. He'll be back soon, he misses the food and his mamma. Then he said he was just across the water, that he could see Sicily. I'd never seen the ocean, what did I know? The desert, I'd never seen a desert either. These letters didn't always come, she said.

What happened then?

She looked away.

Did he go to Australia?

Australia? No, no. She looked worried, glanced around suddenly as if the park were closing in. Not Australia.

I felt my time running out, I had to ask. Did you ever meet anyone after the war that he'd known from the army? Did he ever tell you about anyone he met there?

She shook her head, looking down. It was so long ago. He didn't like to talk about it. She released my hand. I didn't tell him either about the things that happened here while he was away. She met my gaze uncertainly and I could see that the sharpness had worn out of her eyes. I sat back on the bench, looking around the park to distract myself, I was embarrassed by the emotional force of my disappointment. It had been silly to hope that she might have news of a man her dead husband had known sixty years before.

I walked with Pilar as she pushed signora Elena's chair back toward her apartment. You know, Pilar said, when signora Elena was occupied, her face buried in the fluff of a giant white dog, there are some papers, some photographs, in the apartment. I think she doesn't even remember she has them, or she would want you to see. I found them in the desk when I was cleaning, I do the cleaning while signora Elena naps. It's your grandfather you're looking for, yes? Maybe you can come by tomorrow when she is sleeping in the afternoon and look at them. I don't think it will hurt, but if signora Elena is asleep she won't know to mind. She started to tell me about her grandfather, who'd been one of the early members of the

Peruvian National Symphony Orchestra, he'd taught her to play the flute, both the wooden instrument and one made of silver kept in a case that only he was allowed to touch. She spoke of the emails she sent her sister to read to him, but how he was too unwell to speak on the phone. I wonder sometimes, she said, if he's died and no one has told me. I would have gone back for the funeral, those are important to us. But I wouldn't have been able to return here, I don't have the right card. She shrugged, smiling downwards. But who knows? As long as I am in Italy he is alive and my sister reads him my letters. When did your grandfather die?

I wondered when in my Spanish I had implied that I was looking for my grandfather, tried to remember how I'd phrased my research. I paused. Seven years ago, I said finally, which after all was the truth.

Signora Elena's apartment was large and surprisingly dark, given the high ceilings. The windows, instead of filling the rooms with light, emphasized the shadows, the wood-paneled walls and enormous furniture gave a feeling of weight and heft. I could imagine that everything had been laid out in precisely these arrangements for decades, the furniture sinking into the floor so that the wood and tile melded and became one. The desk, a huge sideboard of nearly black wood, dominated the main room over the armchairs and green sofa. Pilar had let me in quietly, turning the knob as she closed the door so that the click was muffled, though it scraped roughly as she shut it. I don't think her sons will mind, she said again, softly, but it takes so long to ask. And they're so far away, they might not understand. She opened a drawer at the bottom of the desk on the left-hand side, took out a small box, and withdrew from it a stack of papers and photographs. I took them from her and sat down on the couch. Pilar remained standing. I looked at the photographs first. A group shot, all the men in uniforms in a desert landscape, Ethiopia or Libya, I was ashamed to not be able to tell the difference, but the cacti next to them looked the same to me as in the American Southwest. Another photo in which a man stood in front of a car with its engine open, clutching a tool, his arm slung around another man, both with cigarettes hanging languidly from their mouths. I looked closely at the second man's face, they both looked young, but the second man looked prepubescent. I could practically see the wispy blond hairs of his upper lip.

Pilar had moved to the kitchen, I could hear her moving around, and I began to read the newspaper clippings, mostly announcements of Italian military victories. Beneath that was a stack of letters, in cramped feminine handwriting, thirty of them or more. I read the top few, slowly and laboriously, on top of the handwriting the dialect was strong, the grammar older and more formal, I barely understood anything. I was guessing at several letters of the alphabet, realized how lucky I was that Loredana's lawyer had typed the military records for me. From what I could tell they were written by signora

Elena, she mostly spoke, I guessed by the nouns, about her mother and his mother, various people who could have been neighbors or siblings, and what food they'd been able to make that week. In the creases inside the envelopes and under the places that stamps must have gone there were scrawled, in even harder-to-read writing, what I came to realize were dirty messages to her husband. I let out a laugh that I then stifled, hoping Pilar hadn't heard. After I read a few of the letters as best I could, I began to flip through envelopes, scanning idly for dates. I wondered what had happened to the letters her husband had written, if she hadn't kept them or if something had happened to them in Rome during the war. He must have brought hers back, keeping them through his time in Australia. Pilar had come back into the room, and just at that moment my hand brushed a letter toward the bottom of the pile that was stiffer than the rest. I pulled it out. The envelope was unlabeled, and it was heavier than the other envelopes. It was stiff because, as far as I could tell, it had never been opened, it was still sealed.

Pilar was watching me, had asked if I was done. Si, I said, not knowing if I was starting a sentence in Spanish or Italian. I was desperate, suddenly, to read the last, unopened letter, but it was clear Pilar was ready for me to go, I didn't want to get her in trouble, and reading the letters had taken so much time, there was no way I'd have time to read this last one before signora Elena woke up. But what kind of a man brought a letter back from the war and kept it for fifty years without ever sending or opening it? Or rather, I thought, what kind of letter?

I stood up, thanking her in Italian for letting me examine the papers, and began to walk them back to the desk. I'd covered the letter with the stack of newspapers when I'd stood up, but I kept my thumb on it as my fingers curled to support the stack. Pilar smiled and held out both hands to take it from me. I smiled back and handed her the top of the stack, with the newspapers and photographs, as if the whole thing were too heavy. When she turned, bending to put them back into their box in the drawer, I slipped the letter under my shirt, a corner tucked into my jeans, and lowered the rest of the pile toward her while she was still bent. I thanked her again, warmly and sincerely, and left the apartment with my bag pressed to my side, holding the letter in place.

I waited until I was safe within the walls of Loredana's apartment to open the envelope. Sitting cross-legged on my bed I cracked the stiff paper with my finger, the glue was so fragile it needed only the suggestion to part. Inside was not a letter but two photographs. In one, a fearsome archangel with six wings loomed down from a mosaic, his beard enormous and his eyes full of rage. The other photograph showed a man in uniform, his face entirely shadowed by the wide brim of his helmet, standing in a field next to a pile of bodies. I knew it was corpses that lay in piles next to the man and behind him, but my conscious mind did not know how I knew, I couldn't see hands or limbs or anything really that was identifiable, only the small dark circles of heads, but I knew on a primal level, as a human being, that what I was looking at were other human beings. I exhaled. In the background, behind these figures, a line of trees faded into a forest.

The photographs were brittle and I tried to touch only the edges as I examined them, afraid they would crumble to dust in my hands. There were no dates, no names, but on the back of the photograph of the angel mosaic, it was a postcard, not a photograph, were written two words, Debre Libanos. When I typed these strange words into Google, pulling myself into the library, my curiosity stronger than my horror, it was immediately in front of me, it was a Christian monastery a few hours north of Addis Ababa, where, in 1937, Italian soldiers had massacred, depending on which sources you credited, either four hundred or two thousand monks, priests, and pilgrims after an assassination attempt on the governor of the colony. They had divided the monks and priests from the others, loaded them onto trucks in groups of thirty to fifty, and driven them to a field, where they were lined up and shot with machine guns. The pilgrims, local families who had come to the monastery to celebrate the feast day of its patron saint, were sent to concentration camps already established for their compatriots in the desert. Only a handful ever returned. The bodies of the holy men were left in piles in a shallow gulley so that, twenty-three days later, a boy from the local village who'd heard the gunfire found them still there, partially eaten by several species of large carnivores now on the verge of extinction.

✣   ✣   ✣

I stood and left the library, still clutching the dry paper in my hand until it crinkled in my grip and the sound returned me to my senses and I returned the photographs neatly to their envelope and stored it in the drawer of my nightstand. My thoughts moved quickly, overwhelmingly, there were dozens more things I needed to look up, the Ethiopian orthodox church, the preceding massacre in the capital, concentration camps, but as I left the apartment building and began to walk south, my thoughts were overrun by the warm, gentle wind, they became blurrier, more languid, and I let myself sink into this state, this muddy pool of thought. What did it mean that signora Elena's husband had kept these souvenirs of the massacre until his death, kept them next to the letters from his wife, what did it mean that the envelope had never been opened? Had he taken the photograph, was he the man pictured, had it been given to him, when would it have been developed? Vietri was too young to have been in Ethiopia, but he'd been in Libya, he might have known signora Elena's husband there, he might have seen these pictures, might have heard the stories. I wandered through neighborhoods I didn't usually visit, my turns were random, but I felt a kind of deep energy that caused me to turn uphill, for example, where I usually would have avoided the slope. I walked, I thought of the bones of the monks in their field, I kept walking.

The summer Andrea and I were thirteen he'd spent devising as many tests as he could for me. This, of course, was how

I thought of it, not that Andrea's motivations were any clearer to me at present. He told me we should visit a church, some excuse, like it was where our grandparents had been married, where my mother had been baptized. He'd laughed when we'd entered the foyer and seen the skeletons looming down, the thighbones protruding from the walls in menacing patterns, arranged by the monks of the order after their brothers' passings. I did my best not to start, and I could tell Andrea was disappointed, he kept pointing to the various posed dead men, one writing with a quill, one sweeping the floor, and asking which one I liked. This one? This one? Your children, they'll be beautiful! He'd added an appreciative hand gesture, here and there. I kept a postcard from the church, a photograph of the bone altar, in my desk drawer through college, it had said something to me about mortality and commitment and groups of men in isolation that I thought might be important to remember.

I thought of the Ethiopian monks, thought of their bones left exposed on the ground until the end of the war. I thought of a twenty-year-old boy with barely a mustache who finds himself in Africa. Was it atonement that Vietri was pursuing through his books? If it was, what could have possibly taken him so long to begin? It had been almost seven decades since the end of that war, millions of lives had already been lived in their completion. Just because he was too young to have been in Ethiopia, just because he wasn't there, he hadn't taken part in this particular massacre, was that better, or was that just luck, how could being absent mean he was innocent? And if it didn't, if he wasn't innocent, what was I doing chasing after him, what was I doing with my years? And if this was his great sin, what was mine?

Sometime before my eleventh birthday, my mother had consulted with herself and decided to taper her medication down to nothing, and she promptly developed the idea that my father was holding my grandfather hostage. She began to retrieve my father's receipts from the trash and write down the mileage in his car each day when he returned home, making circles on maps she would hide in deep in the cabinet under the bathroom sink. My father had pretended not to notice her trips to the garage.

One day she'd picked me up from the fifth grade and drove us out to Yuba City, past the orchards and lazy streams, to towns made up of no more than a grocery store and motel surrounded by almond groves. She checked us into a Motel 6, smiling warmly at the Sikh man behind the front desk. We can trust people with beards, she whispered loudly, and I cringed as he walked us to our room, hoping there was some way he hadn't heard, hoping also that this embarrassment so deep in my middle it felt like dread was of the normal, eleven-year-old variety, like when my friends at school would roll their eyes and call their mothers crazy.

For two days she would only let us eat apples. Fruit is the only thing we can trust, she said. She'd bought several pounds at a farm stand on the way, but she didn't seem to notice the ants that had found a rotting one, deep in the bag, and I cleaned the black line of them as best as I could with toilet paper from the bathroom. I worked on my homework on the bed while she had conversations into the phone, talking strangely, with soups of unrelated words, though I could hear the operator message telling her the numbers she was dialing were no longer in service, and the eventual flat beep, but she would pause to listen as if someone were on the other end. Once, when I thought she was in a good mood, humming to herself, studying a map of Northern California, I'd asked if I could call my dad. Her mood flipped, and she'd unplugged the phone from the wall and clutched it to her breast like a baby.

The third night, when she was deeply asleep for the first time and I was wobbly from hunger, I called my father and told him the name of the motel. That night, after he'd arrived, was the last time I saw my mother outdoors, her hair unbrushed and her eyes furious, red and blue lights behind her, illuminating the almond trees. I fell asleep in my bed after eating half a jar of peanut butter, and when I woke in the morning, my father told me he had surrendered control of my mother to the state of California.

My father deposited her monthly disability check into my bank account, he'd told me once that he'd married her and could pay for her care but that I might as well get something out of her condition, as he called it. It was this money, guilt money, eleven hundred dollars a month, that had, supplemented by my part-time jobs, paid my tuition and rent at Berkeley, that had accumulated while I worked at the bookstore after college, this money that I'd used to travel for these months, that had paid for my hostel bed at fifteen euro a night, and now the room at Loredana's. Sometimes I wished my father would divorce her and start over, try to be happy with someone else, reclaim the life that had been taken from him, but he seemed content to keep her as his anchor, distantly attached, but in the end unreachable.

Chapter Fourteen

I knew it wasn't exactly her area of study, but the next day I texted Anna to ask about the song, "Faccetta Nera," that signora Elena had sung. I'd found videos of it on YouTube, jauntily playing over footage of men dressed in black marching by the thousands, but I wanted context, wanted her decisiveness, her expertise. I didn't tell her about the photographs, out of selfish possessiveness, or because it seemed too hard to explain. Anna wrote back to me as an email within the afternoon, giving me some background on the song, some of the rumors that had swirled at the time as to its inspiration, a young Ethiopian girl. Anna went on to connect it to the painter, as if she knew what I was really after. It's very ironic, she wrote. He was freed from the village because of this victory in Addis Ababa, that's what allowed him to return home to write his book, that's the year the song was the most popular, and it was a fascist song, the message is plainly colonialist. But it didn't take long for a panic to start, for everyone to start fearing that Italy would soon be a country of mixed race. There were never more than twenty families, that is, Italian women, in the new colony, and all those young men singing about the beauty of that girl's black face. So this fear of miscegenation, the alliance with Germany, led to the establishment of the Italian racial laws, which ended up, though it wasn't really the inspiration, having a huge focus on the Jews, and a few years later resulted in the deportations, led ultimately to the painter's death. It's all connected, she ended the email. Stammi bene.

And so I began a period of great research. I tried to read about the Italian campaign in Ethiopia, the one in which the commander had said, simply, chillingly, that his dear duce would "have Ethiopia with or without the Ethiopians," this man, Graziani, who ordered the massacre of thirty thousand civilians in response to a single assassination attempt, the precursor to what happened in the monastery. I read about the battles in the desert, looked up testimonies of Italian prisoners of war sent to England, the language was a suction pulling me under. In a letter sent home from Ethiopia a young man chided himself to his sister over some silly mistake, calling himself "qu'imbecillito io," what a little imbecile I am, and I read the line in Andrea's exact intonation, then immediately shut the book and left it abandoned in the dining room. Often I could only consume a page or two at a time, and then my attention would swerve entirely to focus on something else, a leaf pattern from the sycamore tree above my bench as a shadow on the pavement, a scab on my knee from a mosquito bite. I would think again of California's stunted sycamores, and for the first time I would think it strange that it was California, with all its space, that didn't allow them to grow. I would flinch when I remembered Settimia and her anger, my guilt spiral would lead me to memories of my ex-boyfriend and my shame at what I'd done to him, to wonder about Giancarlo and Laura, more comforting to me were thoughts of Giulia, back now in London, Andrea, whom I hadn't told I'd lost my phone, hadn't given the new number, but who I knew would be waiting. I would seat myself at a desk in the enormous room of a public library and open a volume overfilled with maps and panoramic photographs of alien-seeming desert landscapes rendered in watery, subdued aquamarines, stuffed throughout the pages as though they were the certificates of birth and death throughout a family Bible, and I would pull out a map slowly, but still, in its unfolding, it would split with a crack down the line of one of the folds, a split running halfway down the length, and I would look around furtively, ashamed I had destroyed something so old, then I would remember what I was unfolding was a book of fascist propaganda, the commander's own version of the Ethiopian war published by Mondadori only seven months after its end, a book, it was clear, that no one but myself had opened in fifty years, and I would skim another page or two before giving up and resuming my wandering of the city. I would argue with myself as I walked, I was the one who wanted to know these things, there was no external reason I needed to keep going, and so I would sit down and read another page about the deployment of mustard gas against civilians in Libya, mustard gas, "the closest thing at the time to a weapon of mass destruction," this, obviously, in a different volume, one published after the war, and after reading another half a page about the effects of mustard gas on these civilians, permission for their use asked of the beloved duce on the day after Christmas, I would read about the effects of this gas on Libyan limbs and eyes, the paths of their biologies taking a crooked turn, I would read the memoirs of a pilot who "undertook the war with passion, urgency, cheerfulness," and I would read about the bombing of the sacred Libyan site of Cufra by which "the Italians sought to cancel any rival native history that contested their own." I would read that the main export of Italian-occupied Libya, despite all the years they'd held it, despite the desire to make it once again the breadbasket of the Roman empire, for the greatness of the past they wanted was not the greatness of Garibaldi, of Risorgimento, was not even the Renaissance, it was Rome they wanted, and yet in all the years they held Libya the main export was not grain, or even oil, but salt. Salt! And I would close the book. I realized it was silly how I had left things with Settimia, I didn't understand what could have possessed me to not want to go to lunch with her, did I really think I could face all of this alone? But of course it was one thing to realize this, and another to build up the courage to act. I thought I should call Andrea and ask what he and his friends were doing that night, I wanted to drink a never-ending glass of wine among a huge group of raucous people my own age in which I could laugh and only half follow conversations and never talk except to say perfectly that my Italian wasn't very good and I preferred to listen while I let the waves of vowels pass over me. But it was 2011, there was a crisis, no one my age had any money, and anyway, Italians never got drunk. I would call Andrea soon, I knew, and in the meantime I decided to feed my solitude while I could, and so I walked the city accompanied only by my thoughts, returning eventually to Loredana's, to my small quiet room, the room that was only mine and mine alone.

By a few afternoons later my decision had gathered sufficient strength and I texted Settimia a message of apology and warmth and it was arranged that I would come to dinner, I would get to meet Dida's baby, she was now back in Rome. I brought Loredana, escorting her slowly by the arm into the apartment Dida and her fiancé had rented near the Piazza Bologna. Dida had turned into a sharp-faced, blunt-haircutted woman whose severe features frequently exploded into laughter. She was so joyful, cheerfully declaring she was too young to have a baby, casually pulling aside her wrap dress to feed him, leaning into her fiancé, a Frenchman, while she did so, happily directing her mother and Giulia, in town for the weekend, around her apartment, which, while neither as large nor as old as our grandfather's, had something that jogged at my memory, or maybe it was just these people, this specific combination of voices. Dida's sister, Clea, was there, as was their father, my grandmother's brother Bipo. Bipo was the only other sibling from their side who had come to Rome, and he sat with his wife, my aunt Eta, and Andrea's father, Giacomo, kindly in the corner. Bipo was almost a decade younger than my grandmother, had been born after the war, and was treated by everyone, even his daughters, as the harmless baby brother that he was. He asked me how my parents were doing and I told him they were well, caught Clea looking at her mother out of the corner of my eye. Loredana had settled comfortably on the couch next to Settimia, and she was easy around them, but stayed close to me. I was mildly surprised that my not residing with some member of the family had not been a source of contention, but it seemed everyone considered the connection with Loredana enough, everyone of the previous generation, I realized, remembered Benedetta well. The whole family acted as if I'd just returned to Rome, no one brought up my presence in the city before this evening, not even Andrea, in the kitchen with Fahad, at work on a South Asian dessert involving rose petals.

Dida's fiancé, Jean-Luc, insisted on bringing Loredana and me to the rooftop to see the sunset, and we watched as the shadows increased across the buildings, the river and postcarded landmarks invisible from our angle, so that it could have been any European city of terra-cotta rooftops and occasional wide avenues, hills framing the distance. He and Dida had met in Paris, where she'd gone for a year of postgraduate study. The baby's name was Henri. They were planning a wedding, but maybe in a few years when they could afford a big one. We chatted in Italian, it had been so long since I'd spoken French, I imagined it would be gluey on my tongue, and I didn't want to exclude Loredana. He worked for some kind of IT company. The baby was neither exactly planned nor exactly unplanned. He liked Rome. We went back inside and I sat next to Dida and she smiled at me and asked if I wanted to hold the baby, but he began to fuss and she took him to another room and put him to bed, returning half an hour later with a look of content exhaustion.

I took Loredana home in a taxi and helped her into the apartment. When we'd said our goodbyes at the door to Dida's apartment, I understood that I was back in the family fold, they all had my cell phone number now, I would be absorbed. Somehow, the thought did not spark the panic I thought it would.

Chapter Fifteen

The next morning I decided to write down everything I knew about Vietri. I loved lists, their orderliness and the way they offered up a clear set of tasks, breaking down the world into smaller and smaller parts, when my thinking tended to the expansive, to the currents, not to the details. I felt spun out of control by the reestablishment in my life of so many family members all at once, and I wanted an anchor, I wanted a path that was mine. So far the quest to find Vietri had gained me only fragments, I felt adrift, I had glimpses of stories, but they did not cohere into a whole. How were these things, Vietri's book orders, the painter and his lonely death, the massacre of the monks in Debre Libanos, how were these part of the same world, how would they ever be one narrative?

These were the facts I knew:

1. Giordano Vietri was born in Aliano in 1920.

2. He may or may not have known the painter during the time of the painter's exile in Aliano, from the years 1935 to 1936, when Vietri was fifteen to sixteen.

3. He joined the army in 1940, was sent to Ravenna and then to Libya, to Tobruk and then to El Alamein.

4. In Libya, he was in the unit of signora Elena's husband.

5. All of the Italian troops in Africa had either been killed, deserted, or become English prisoners of war. Vietri had become a prisoner of war.

6. His last known address, in the year 2008, was on the via Bevanda, where hundreds of books were shipped to him by a bookstore in Berkeley. By me.

The rest was a blank. My mind settled into the gap between the last two items, what had happened to him after Africa? The foglio matricolare declared "prigioniero di guerra degli Inglesi in A.S. 6 Febbraio, 1941," but there was no information about where he had been sent, how he had returned to Italy, what had happened to him after the war. A government website confirmed that only a small portion of the records the British had kept on their prisoners of war were digitized, and none were searchable by name. It was a dead end, unless I wanted to go to England and spend years combing the lists of prison camp residents hoping to see the familiar letters, terrified my attention would slip at just the wrong moment and I would pass over, never knowing how close I'd come. Not to mention those captured in Africa weren't all sent to England, not only to Australia, like signora Elena's husband, but also to South Africa, India, the US, all were possibilities, he could have gone anywhere in the empire of the British and their allies, and those were the years when the "sun never set" on them.

I googled listlessly. How would I find the thread in the postwar years? I felt that morning how deeply this was a foreign country, a foreign language, and I felt a sense of despair and alienation come on so fast it was as if I'd been thrown into an ocean. I could be here for years before I was fluent, and it wasn't just the looking, it was the knowing how to look. I tried to imagine what it would have been like if I had continued my summers in Rome, I mourned this other self, imagined a life in which I felt at home in this city, fluent in Italian, in which my cousins and I knew about one another's wardrobes and boyfriends, interests and fears. For the first time, I wondered if this fear I had of being like my mother, of being, I made myself think the word, schizophrenic, was something the others in my generation of my family shared. I'd never thought to look up the chance of a niece or nephew, a second or third cousin, inheriting it. Had this shadow been here, even in Rome? Had it haunted Dida's pregnancy? Part of me had always believed that it was a sickness of California, of its idealism and naivete, its rootlessness and sun, the long expanse narrowed between mountains and ocean. How could it have happened to my mother in Rome, there was no space, no room for it to have taken root, no quiet afternoons for it to have begun its creep, no solitude where thoughts could betray you. If I let myself be reabsorbed into this Roman family, would I be safe? Or would I simply remind them that they themselves were not safe, would I be a reminder to my aunts, a threat to my cousins, a specter to haunt this new generation?

I'd already rejected the quiet, easy life I'd slipped into after college, the one I'd left for my months of restless travel. Was that now over? I'd now been in Rome longer than I'd been in any other city. I was running out of lives I could pursue in my twenties, there were few directions left in which to swerve. This search for Vietri was a non sequitur, a jump out of the narrative, but I was afraid for it to be over, because then I would need to choose a new life, a new mode of moving through the world, and now I was twenty-five. I felt strongly that whatever I did next would need to propel me through my thirties, but *a woman's risk extends to the age of thirty*, it might not matter. I didn't know how to decide what did matter. What had Vietri done with his years? Why had he stopped ordering from the store? What had he done with those books, where had he taken them? What had he learned, and what had I hoped to learn from him? I was beginning to worry that my search would never have a body, a conclusion. Instead of the mystery narrowing to a solution, a culprit, Colonel Mustard, in the conservatory, at five o'clock in the evening, with a lead pipe, for reasons of inheritance, it would expand outward like an inverted cone. The things I could know about a life were nearly infinite, I could go on collecting knowledge of Vietri for years, there would always be gaps, there would always be something I didn't know, or failed to understand. The question was beginning to lurk in the periphery of my thoughts, when would I be done? And that other question, the propeller of all Italian conversational narrative, arose: E poi? And then?

In the end I reread the business profile of the pottery company bearing his surname I had found my first week in Rome, the one that had mentioned a Giordano present at the founding of the company, and decided to look into it. I didn't know how Vietri could have been involved in the founding of the company that bore his name without leaving any trace of his presence, didn't know how likely it was that this Giordano was the Giordano Vietri I searched for, but what else did I have to do, I found the email of the journalist who had written the article and asked if he would meet me for a drink.

He, Roberto, arrived at the bar only fifteen minutes late, older than I was by perhaps a decade, stocky without having any extra weight, his dark hair curly with narrow lines of gray I could tell had just begun to appear. He came up so confidently to my table that I could only imagine how American I looked, though we'd emailed in Italian and he might have been expecting a boy. We ordered beers, which I paid for. I had told him of my interest in the article in my initial email and I asked him, once the waiter had returned with the drinks, if he had met everyone he'd interviewed for it, specifically the man named Giordano he'd quoted, if he had recorded his full name. I'd printed out a copy of the article at an internet café as if it were a homework assignment, afraid he wouldn't remember, it had been written over half a decade before, and I took it out, a bit embarrassed, but he took it from me eagerly and, I flattered myself, appreciatively. He read through efficiently, taking quick sips of his beer, his elbow out at an energetic angle. He finished, folded the paper and returned it to me, then extracted a small notebook from his pocket, these are my notes from that time, he shrugged with a smile. I felt my lips part. Roberto was charming, in the way some Italians have of making you want to help them though nothing they've said is particularly out of the ordinary. Roberto had that quality, that rush-over-to-the-cute-toddler-and-pay-attention-to-him magnetism. I suppose it must have been helpful in his career. I was not immune to it, though I distrusted it.

I spoke with him on the phone, Roberto continued, it was when I was first in Rome, I was just starting out, this is the type of piece I would do. His next sip was apologetic. They weren't important enough for face-to-face interviews, proba-bly they were all phone calls. I didn't record his last name, usu-ally that's because the person asks me not to, though I don't remember why this would have been the case. I was disap-pointed and then ashamed of myself for this disappointment, of course he hadn't met Vietri, of course he couldn't tell me if it even was Vietri he'd spoken to. I still had yet to meet anyone who'd met him. He seemed to sense my deflation, which made me feel embarrassed, and summarized the rest of the notes for me in some detail, the Giordano of the article had been work-ing as a laborer in Ostia, he'd had a chance encounter with the American women who'd wanted to found the company. It was common at the time, still even now, Roberto said, for companies owned by foreigners to need to have someone on the ground to help with the shipping and customs, things like that. I asked what his voice had sounded like, and he said it was soft, an accent from the south. I wasn't sure if Roberto was making any of that up, it seemed a lot of detail for the sparse amount of words written on the page, but I was grateful.

Shall we get another round? he asked, and I nodded, he was already gesturing to the waiter. I was finding Roberto that rare thing, that creature I hadn't encountered since arriving in Rome, an enjoyable drinking companion. He had a looseness that was rare for Romans, and I asked where he was from. Brescia, he said. It's in the north. Why are you interested in this man? He turned to examine me. I thought it was the company you were interested in, maybe because you are American, but it's this man, yes? Do you know him?

No, I said. Or, not really. We corresponded a few years ago, I was helping him to order academic books from the US, and when I got to Rome, I wanted to meet him, but I couldn't find him. I just wanted to find out about his life . . . I shrugged. I started, and now I feel like I have to finish.

He nodded as the waiter placed the new beers before us. There are stories like that. Usually it's that you need something about the world explained to you. You want to understand the order of things and you think that if you trace the life of this man it will do that for you. You are Italian, yes? Your family? I nodded, hesitating only slightly. So you come, and you want a way to find the history you think you missed. Usually people look for their own grandparents, great-grandparents. He looked at me sharply. Is he your grandfather, some relative? I shook my head slowly. Roberto's quick movements, his energy, seemed to foster the opposite in me, and I could feel how languidly I moved, reacted, how hesitating I was when I spoke. He moved sharply, his body was like a knife, he spit his words like they were darts. I felt as if he could split me. I asked if he'd had a story like that. He nodded. Of course. It's something you have to learn as a journalist, he said, breaking eye contact. When to let a story go.

The next afternoon I went back to Dida's apartment. As I'd suspected, now that my cell phone number was family property, I was at the mercy of these invitations, and I was surprised how little I minded. Andrea had helped me decipher his own texts at the beginning of my time in Rome, the code of *x*'s and *k*'s and numbers that transubstantiated into other words when spoken out loud in Italian, so that I knew enough by now how to answer "6 lib?" and I was always free. Perversely, I liked to text in full, grammatically correct sentences, which I knew annoyed Andrea, but I felt it was my right to claim this one way of expressing correct Italian, when I could write it out and check for errors. I'd been quite proud of the email I'd sent Roberto, it had been my first opportunity to write a full paragraph, and I'd felt during our drinks that he had been convinced in advance of my seriousness. That morning, Dida had sent me a squillo, she'd let my cell phone ring once and hung up, a way of saying hello, or that she was thinking of me. I knew enough now to never pick up the phone unless someone called twice, a legacy of the minute plan when the call was free unless you answered, but I still wasn't totally sure how to interpret this new idiom, so I'd sent her a text back, and anyway, here I was going over to see the baby.

On my previous visit he'd alternated between sleeping and

breastfeeding, and now that he was awake and unattached, he was in a particularly gurgly lie-on-your-back stage, I could see that his eyes were a deep blue, the features of his face un-fixed as if pushed gently out of clay. Dida smiled whenever she looked down at him but was openly more interested in com-plaining about Jean-Luc's difficulty in finding work in Rome. Everything here is connections, she repeated often as if it were a form of punctuation. I'd assumed his job was a reason they had moved back, but in fact it seemed that the work he had was part-time or freelance, I could never quite parse the Ital-ian economy, anyway Dida complained about "contracts." She herself was working part-time for a publisher, a job she'd got-ten through a high school friend. You must know, she said. I made a vague gesture, embarrassed to tell her plainly that I hadn't really attempted to look for work in Rome, I had no de-sire to nanny for an American family or teach English to busi-ness students, I found it easier just to not spend any money and live within my monthly deposit. I assured her it was bad in the US as well, the economy had crashed a few months after I'd graduated and the microgeneration I inhabited was divided by the sharp line of that September. But you value the young, she said. No one here thinks you have anything to contribute until you're forty, but we can see plainly that there will be nothing left for us if we wait our turn. You know that woman who married your grandfather still collects his pension. She fixed me with a stare, and I nodded, acknowledging that she would probably do so for another forty years. Jean-Luc talks about going to Dubai, Dida continued, you can have a good life there. She checked her phone and announced casually that Clea was on her way over to see me, and I decided not to bring up my objections to the labor practices of the Emirates.

Clea showed up with her boyfriend, Marco. They had been together for four years, though they didn't live together, she still lived with her parents, and so did he. Of course they wanted to join the conversation I'd begun with Dida, the favorite topic of Italians my age, I was learning, was their morose but not unfounded fatalism about the life that was possible for them. Marco spoke of the high turnover rate among his fellow journalists. A lot of my friends have become chefs, he said almost wistfully, and I could see it sparked a panic in Clea. She had maintained her white-hot energy since we were younger, and argued with him, they must have had this conversation before, possibly they were having it again using simplified language for my benefit.

What I loved about the young people my age, I thought while their debate continued, was that no one asked me what I did all day. I had expected to be embarrassed, but I had slowly observed that no one my age had full-time employment, this was an economy of freelancers and temporary part-time workers, if they weren't lucky enough to still be in school like Andrea. No one called Clea a lawyer, she "had a law degree." Everyone my age understood how easy it was to loaf away the hours, especially, I could see, with these visits, so that seeing one member of my family turned most often into a full reunion, every meal set for a dozen people. Even with small tasks, the conversion of time was twenty to one, anything that took five minutes in California was an hour in Rome, I remembered in my teenage summers spending a full hour buying ibuprofen for my cramps, first finding a pharmacy that was open, then waiting patiently for the pharmacist to wrap the box in paper and tie it with ribbon, curling the ends.

The conversation went on, propelled by Marco's frequent jokes, he flung some in my direction and I would laugh. I liked Marco, but was uneasy with his ease, I still had not found my balance vis-à-vis the male-female nonrelational friendship in Rome, was it okay for me to be friendly with him in front of Clea? Clea wasn't as straightforward as Dida, she could hide her emotions, I didn't want to offend her, my last foray into such a friendship, with Giancarlo and Laura, I had destroyed spectacularly, and I felt a pang of regret. The ease of traveling, which comes from leaving behind any problems you create, was no longer with me in Rome. I supposed I was going to have to learn from my mistakes and try hard not to repeat them.

Chapter Sixteen

A few days later I had occasion to revisit a memory from the bookstore, a memory that was precious to me, and so one that I rarely thought about. It had been a Saturday, which, given our reliance on the campus community, was always a quiet day in the store, and I was up at the front desk, observing the minutes pass slowly. There was only one customer, a woman in perhaps her early sixties with blonde hair that blurred seamlessly into gray, cut like a helmet in the protective way of academics of a certain generation, who had headed to the more obscure subject sections on the mezzanine. She approached with her purchase after an hour or so, with a wry smile that bordered on exasperation, and I braced myself, I never knew what mood of a customer I would need to absorb. The book she handed me was a volume on Dante, priced at over a hundred dollars, one of those volumes put out by university presses that they expect exactly thirty-five people or libraries in the world to buy, and when I told her the total with tax, she shook her head mournfully. I shouldn't be buying this, she said matter-of-factly, but when I read the dedication, she continued, I found I had to. She opened to the page and pushed the book gently toward me on the counter. "To Peter," it read, "il sole dei miei occhi." The sun of my eyes, I said. She smiled at me, completely unsurprised that I had been able to read the Italian, and I smiled back, feeling blessed by the sentence's grace.

I hadn't thought of this woman for years, not even when I'd encountered the occasional Dante impersonators blown south from Florence, leering through their white paint, until one afternoon, momentarily blinded as I came from behind the pillar of a fountain on a hill with the city and the midday light below, that phrase arose, "il sole dei miei occhi," and I think only then did I truly realize what it meant.

I began to see Roberto. Suddenly the unending time I'd had, the long afternoons and evenings of reading and walking, content in my solitude, were no longer mine. Everyone in Rome was wonderful at loafing away time, relocations, breaks at home, tardiness, somehow a whole week was lunch with Loredana, a spritz with Andrea and Fahad, or Clea and Marco, parading the baby around a park with Dida, Sunday dinner at Settimia and Giacomo's, Roberto now filling in the gaps. We proceeded slowly, we were cautious with each other, often he joined me for my long walks after he was done at the office, or for a midday break. My relationships with my family, in contrast, expanded exponentially, once I'd been admitted into one person's life, their whole friend group was opened up to me, they seemed not to have in their possession the concept of an invite list, or rather, not inviting every intimate to every gathering. But their friend groups were all decades old, from childhood, I was exempt only because I was family, a term that could stretch as far as one needed. There were no divisions, all of my Roman selves, all of the different selves I had had with different people, I could see now they were all merging into one person.

I found Roberto waiting for me outside of Loredana's later that week, leaning against the building, smoking a cigarette with no discernable enjoyment. I smiled and leaned into the kisses he placed on my cheeks. In the daylight I could see the difference in our ages, his face had lines mine had not yet developed. He'd mentioned, during our first conversation, that he'd been frequently away from Rome for the last two years, often in Sicily. Another time he'd said that he hadn't been back to the north in five years. Surprised, I'd asked if his parents were still there, and he shook his head. So, he was usually boisterous, but he had his silences. This night, I could tell he was frustrated, restless, as the late-afternoon light changed to orange of Campari in our spritzes, which he insisted on referring to as pirlos, his one Brescian trait. I asked him what he was working on and he mentioned something about a migrant center, stopped himself, then told me I didn't want to know. I withdrew my hand from his arm, which he caught, apologetic. He gave me a weary smile. It's just, I will work on this for years, and nothing will ever happen, most people will never go to trial. They'll make deals, find a way out, make the right compromises with the right people. Most of these things, these corruption investigations, most of the evidence has even been recorded, it's just a matter of obtaining the records. There are records for everything, we have a mania for bureaucracy, I bet you every name in Italy is in a document like this somewhere. But it doesn't mean anyone is punished, that anything changes, even that we can publish anything. He tried to smile. Let's talk about something else.

But I leaned into him. How do you get these records? My search for Vietri was more or less at a standstill, my recent days had been so full he had been away from my thoughts, but I was intrigued by the existence of any files that might have caught his name. Is there a database? I asked, and Roberto made the laughing sound he made when I'd exposed myself as very American. Seeing my expression, he pulled me to him and kissed my temple. I'll tell you, he murmured into my ear, his hand against the side of my face. I have a mentor who calls it the human touch, he said, upon releasing me. Usually, it's best to meet with the prosecutor for coffee or a dinner. You have these relationships for years, you can't just find someone out of the blue. They have all the power, but they will never give you the documents themselves. If you're lucky, they'll ask if you've met a certain person, a clerk, a carabiniere, and that person will be the one with the document you need. Sometimes there are five or six of these links, these meetings. It's all relationships, you always need permission from the person you know to contact the next person, you can never go directly. What do they get out of it? I asked. My belief in humanity's innate sense of justice had been weakened over the past weeks of my historical research. I've thought a lot about that, Roberto said. Sometimes it's revenge, it's personal, and sometimes there really are whistleblowers who want to act for good in the world. But for most people, I think, these men and women are office workers, they're removed from these important processes even if they are instrumental to it. Sometimes I think it's nothing more than a desire to have a hand in something bigger than themselves, to affect the world in some dramatic way. Like the people who leaked the Berlusconi documents, to open the newspaper and see a powerful man brought down and know they had a hand it in. I think what people want sometimes is a connection to the narrative of history, though they are stuck in the present. You know?

In fact there was a kind of database, or something like it. Clea had access to it with her law certification and passed me her credentials without comment. Vietri's name appeared in connection with a trial in the early '80s, he'd been listed as a witness but had never testified, the trial had been scheduled but had never taken place. The record listed one other witness, when I looked him up I found he was a communist of some notoriety who had passed away the year before. Roberto had found his nephew for me, had even located his number and helped me to set up the meeting. I'd planned to refrain from gloating when I told Roberto about the existence of the database, but when I told him, he said, that isn't what you asked about. He seemed perplexed at even the suggestion.

The communist's nephew insisted on meeting me in a nightclub on the outskirts of Rome, my taxi ride was exorbitant. It had been built in the '70s, he explained as he led me through the club, clearly he was comfortable in this environment, he was practically giving me a tour, telling me about how it had been built by avant-garde architects attempting to make the nightclub a total art experience, including music, writing, visual arts, a vegetable garden, he shrugged as we pressed ourselves through bodies. It was crowded, a Friday, when I'd called the day before I'd said that I could only meet him the next night, for some reason I'd felt like being difficult. Though I knew to be grateful to Roberto for setting up the meeting, I was impatient with this next clue, I still wanted the assorted facts I'd learned about Vietri to cohere into a life. The nephew hadn't been bothered, he'd said he had some business, but I could accompany him, and the employees did seem to know him as he led us to a small table in the back, where he asked quickly for a gin, and I asked for one with tonic. Once, he told me as a way to open the conversation, surveying the room, this club was held up by Sardinian shepherds. He didn't elaborate on the story. Our drinks arrived, carried by a waitress with eyes so dark you couldn't see her pupils.

My companion had very dark gray hair streaked occasionally with brilliant veins of white, and his forehead and face protruded as his hairline receded, giving him a look that was permanently anxious, his thick eyebrows jumped rather than moved. I asked him to tell me about the trial, I had told Roberto to tell him it was what I wanted to talk to him about, so I'd been ready for him to be ready to launch into a monologue. But he was able to talk about the legal matter, as he called it, for nearly fifteen minutes uninterrupted by my questions or his own pauses without giving me any real sense of what the crime was or any of the details were. We were speaking Italian, he didn't speak English, and while I knew all of the words he was using, he wasn't speaking Romanesco though he'd used it with the waitress, none of these words were solid nouns, and I had the feeling the phrases he chose were suggestive of other things I was missing in my literal translations. Roberto had offered to accompany me, and I regretted not accepting his offer, I was completely lost in the vagueness, my confidence in my Italian was evaporating rapidly into the sweaty air. I could gather that there was some sort of work, some organization that his uncle had been involved in, but he wasn't there, he kept repeating, but where, I kept asking, nothing was ever resolved. The more I tried to clarify what had actually happened, if the organization was the communist party, no, the Red Brigades, no, the less precise his sentences became. But I don't understand, I said at last, and he nodded, accepting this reality. Sergio only died a year ago, he said, sipping his gin, what bad luck you have. He brought the glass to his mouth while keeping eye contact, so that I didn't believe he thought my luck was bad at all, and I wondered what sort of underworld I had opened up, and how far into it I could proceed before it would be too late to turn back.

You know, he said, just as I'd thought our conversation was over, I was sad, embarrassed, and ready to leave these beautiful people to their dancing, you know it's the fault of your country. Italy was the battleground in those years, and it was you and Russia pouring in fuel. Do you know what I mean by fuel, eh? Money. We say years of lead, but it was money, even that vapid Russian book. There were three thousand murders in those years, political murders. And what have you ever heard about it? My lips parted. They don't teach you that in school there, do they? He had slipped into Romanesco, he brushed his nose as he inhaled sharply, and I wondered if he was drunk already, or high. I felt claustrophobic, with the loud music, the dim lights, the bodies crushing against one another. My companion had fallen silent, looking moodily into his drink, but I felt no urge to defend myself, or my country, even to point out that this was also my country, and I was doing my best to absorb its traumas.

I had continued helping myself to the library of Loredana's husband, somehow I'd started reading an account of the classical docks at Ostia, where according to Roberto's interview the Giordano that might be Vietri worked millennia later. Despite the fact that the ancient iteration of Rome had reached a million people, a number not matched again by a metropolis until London in 1800, it had been an illogical place to build a city, fifteen miles upstream of a fast-flowing river, the mouth of it so silted that goods needed to be loaded and unloaded onto several different vessels along the journey. Two-thirds of the ancient Roman diet was imported grain stored in warehouses throughout the city, and when the Tiber flooded, as it did every twenty years or so, the grain molded and the people died of famine. There were jobs, then, for laborers, most of the importing costs were for dockworkers. Each emperor resolved to expand the port of Rome, each faced the same engineering problem and failed to solve it. It reminded me of a joke popular in the multinational hostels of South America, each country had a slightly different version, where in heaven the French were the cooks, the Germans the engineers, the British the police, and the Italians the lovers; in hell the British were the lovers, the Germans the cooks, the French the police, and the Italians the engineers.

I'd called the PR department of the pottery company, telling them I was a writer based in Rome and asking for more details about the founding of the company. The extremely pleasant woman directed me cheerily to the "our story" page on their website as if I had not thought to read it, in fact I hadn't, which told the story of three American southern women captivated by the patterns on their dinnerware on a visit to the Amalfi Coast in the mid-'80s, saying the name came from one of the towns there, Vietri sul Mare. She said she was sorry she couldn't share any more details.

I was again finding it difficult to talk to my cousins, it wasn't that we'd run up against the limits of my Italian, it was more that our senses of humor, our essential outlooks, seemed to exist on alternate planes. Even as teenagers they had a reserved, ironic attitude toward life that guarded against silliness and openness, they were always sincere, but there was a distance, sometimes in those years I got the feeling their verbal repartee was practiced, that every night they retired to their rooms to ruminate over the best way to phrase a cutting but still jovial remark about the other's new haircut while I, bewildered, observed it all. It wasn't just that it was nearly impossible not to be

totally earnest in a language in which one lacked secure foot-
ing, it was not only that I couldn't make a joke, that Everest of
language learners, that I couldn't pull off sarcasm or irony, it
was also that I was Californian, a cutting remark I didn't mean
would have been the greatest violation of my inner code. The
furthest I'd gotten toward a shared humor was a running joke
in our teenage years where s'okay, which slipped easily from
my mouth, meant it's not okay, in the function of the Italian
commencing s. I was still proud of that one and had tentatively
revived it on one of our recent evenings.

But would I stay? It hadn't yet occurred to me to decide if
I liked Rome. My cousins had no feelings about it, they were
so utterly of it. Loredana, I gathered, did not like the city, but
had long ago accepted it as her fate. Roberto loved Rome, it
had, he said, claiming to be quoting Pasolini, the perfect mixture of beauty and ugliness. He was more connected to the
violence of the city than I was, was updated by his colleagues
daily on the bodies found in the Tiber. That Roberto's job was
important made him all the more alien to me, and I wondered
more and more if he took me seriously at all, at times I thought
of course he didn't, I was an unemployed American a decade
younger not even fluent in his language. We hadn't yet slept together, and I was unused to evaluating boys' interest in myself
without seeing them at their most vulnerable. But sometimes,
I tried to be objective, he did look at me with a hungry interest I didn't think was only sexual. His kisses were earnest, he
would grip my hips tightly, but we were never alone together
in private, we hadn't made an effort to make the opportunity

occur. I was unsure how to proceed, I didn't really know the rules, I could feel my impatience brewing, worried I would act out soon to force things to some sort of breaking point, sex hovered between us, it fueled our walks and our conversations.

I dressed well around Roberto, Dida had given me a few dresses, matter-of-fact about the changes pregnancy had brought to her body, they would now look better on me, and so I should have them. Agnieszka had even stopped short to declare one of them "super cute!," her highest form of praise. I'd bought good leather flats and a vintage purse at the Porto Portese market, where I ended up many Sundays. My bargaining skills had been honed in South America, and I enjoyed putting them to use, even Loredana had been impressed. I had an innate Californian fear of being overdressed, but I had reluctantly relearned that, here, dressing well was a matter of respect. I couldn't be as flamboyant as most of the Roman women I saw, heels were beyond me, but I did make an effort, did sadly discard some of my travel-worn t-shirts and my leather flip-flops, one of whose sole had finally worn through, bidding them a secret, elaborate farewell at the trash can as if releasing their corpses into the ocean in a Viking funeral, a gift for some other world. I'd also bought tights, the most conscious acknowledgment that I would be staying in Rome for the new season, spending those six euro at H&M felt like the most momentous decision I'd made since my arrival in the city. And, thinking of Roberto, I'd bought new underwear.

Roberto knew my whole family situation, of course he did, trying to hide the details, the geography of that particular landscape, would have been like trying to keep a secret where I'd gone to college, I suppose I could have done it, but it would have taken a level of diversion and secrecy I no longer had the energy to perform. After I'd finished telling him about my mother, but before I'd brought up the statistics that haunted me, he said, well, it must be hard to be so different from her, which knocked the breath out of me and made me hide my face in my glass. Anyway, I didn't even have the more traumatic family story. Roberto's father had lost a leg in the '70s when an anti-fascist demonstration he'd attended was bombed, his father's anger had been like a veil over his whole life, and he'd lost his mother to cancer while he was at university in Bologna. Still, there was a tenderness when he spoke of him, this legless, widowed father he hadn't seen in five years, one I didn't understand.

What I wanted to know was the story that Roberto had mentioned, the one he couldn't let go. I searched online for his byline, but never opened the articles, it felt like a betrayal, it was unearned. I had absorbed so many of the stories of others—Maria's, Benedetta's, the painter's, Anna's, the communist's, my mother's story underlying them all—I felt full to the brim, I walked unsteadily holding a bowl that threatened to spill over, the surface was calm, but these unrelated stories churned next to one another underneath. And yet none of them was Roberto's story, none of them was Vietri's story, and none of them, none of these stories, was mine.

Chapter Seventeen

Settimia and I were now taking walks together a few evenings a week. I met her when she was off work in the park outside her office, where she would change her heels into one of several pairs of flamboyantly colored tennis shoes. Our talks would range on these evenings, but mostly they were taken up with the ten years of family news I had missed: I hadn't known, and wanted to now, about Dida's scoliosis in high school, Bipo's recent health scares, the series of career moves that had brought Giulia to London. Even the legal case surrounding my grandfather's apartment, I'd vaguely known that it had dragged on for years after his death, but I had been in college, it was *Bleak House* as far as I was concerned, but here, I did want to know what the various judges had concluded, which was ultimately not in the sisters' favor, but they'd felt vindicated anyway, having made their point in an official capacity. We also talked about my mother, I left alone the sharp memories of my childhood, but I told her about the facility she lived in now, I calmly answered her questions about doctors and treatments. On these walks the October wind moved kindly in the trees over our heads, and it was hard for me to argue with the importance of the world in front of me.

Settimia was easy to talk to, she had the sharp opinions of every Roman, but, what a difference it made, I was automatically included by her inside the veil separating the family from the rest of the world, once I had accepted my place there all of my actions were to be defended, not questioned. The week before, at dinner, I'd made a comment to Clea about some of the boys I'd known in the hostels, not realizing Settimia had turned to listen. After Settimia had given me a kind smile and went into the kitchen, Clea, seeing my face full of horror and embarrassment, had said helpfully, she understands. I decided I had no choice but to act like this was true.

On one of our walks I asked Settimia about Fahad. Did his family know about Andrea? Would he stay in Italy? He's been here for seven years now, she said, after a few moments of thought. We paused at the crest of a small hill, and she materialized a small handkerchief with which she dabbed her forehead before taking out a small compact and reapplying her lipstick. I think it would be hard for him, to go back. But we don't know. He is still on a student visa. Of course Andrè will be very sad if he goes back. But Andrè is still so young. Maybe it would be better.

I was surprised by this, Settimia always had such warmth toward Fahad, but I had underestimated the standards of the Italian mother. I confessed to her then that I didn't feel young, though I was the same age as Andrea, I felt ancient. I felt that I'd already exhausted all of the lives available to me, that the changes needed to get me where I wanted to be, and I didn't even know where that was, were insurmountable, I didn't see how they could ever take place. Settimia didn't laugh at me, just said, simply, it's easier to see the accumulation of small bits of progress when you are my age, it's true, but that doesn't mean it can't happen.

It was in Sicily, Roberto told me, I'd finally asked him. We had walked to the river from his office, he'd just gotten off work, and we sat on a bench overlooking the water. It was one of the last days, I thought, where we would be able to stay outside, it was already on the verge of being too cold. I intertwined my fingers with Roberto's and pressed them together. I had gone there to interview the refugees in the camps, he said, turning to me seriously, I heard a lot of things there I will never forget, and he began to recite them as if they were a list, as if there were images in the camera of his mind, stories he could purge by imparting them into my brain. The boat of migrants, mostly refugees culled from the edges of the Mediterranean by the Arab Spring, deliberately rammed by smugglers once they were sufficiently offshore, they'd wanted to turn around, start a new trip; the woman, eight months pregnant, who was to be rescued first from a boat minutes away from sinking, who in climbing to the rescuer's boat lost her balance and fell between the two vessels and drowned or was crushed; another boat whose engine broke down a quarter of a mile from the coast of the new continent, and since there was no service on any of their phones someone lit a blanket on fire to signal for rescue, but the blanket fire spread to spilled gasoline from the engine and in order to avoid the fire all of the passengers went to the other side of the boat, causing it to capsize, and even though they were so close to shore, almost none of them could swim, over three hundred people had drowned; and then there were the people they pulled from the water suffering not only from hypothermia, exhaustion, but also from various everyday illnesses, colds, the flu, a surprising number from the chicken pox.

But the story I couldn't let go of, he continued, was told to me in Greece by a Palestinian boy who'd befriended an Egyptian law student on the boat, the Egyptian boy had left law school without telling his family in order to go to Europe to earn money, he wanted to pay for a heart treatment needed by his father and he'd decided the family couldn't wait for him to graduate and find a job in Egypt, especially with the situation there. Their boat left from Egypt, after it sank they clung to a life buoy together for almost two days. The Egyptian boy succumbed to exhaustion a few hours before they were rescued, and the Palestinian boy, just a teenager, was so traumatized he couldn't remember his friend's last name. Just Ahmed, from Cairo. So his family, the father he wanted to save, they still don't know, to them he just disappeared. I tried to find out more about this Ahmed, I wanted to let his family know what had happened to him. I spent a week interviewing everyone else who'd survived that boat, searching for Ahmeds from Cairo on the social networks, asking Egyptians who came through on later boats if they'd met him. But I never found out who he was, I was never able to tell his family.

And you know, he continued after a pause, my hands were on his thighs, it won't stop. It's only going to get worse. The fishermen there now call it the season. There are so many people who want to come.

There was a look in Roberto's eyes I wanted to absorb into my body, the look of someone in a dark room so long they can't bear to lift their eyes to the light, and by the end of his litany I knew this was the day I would sleep with him. It was still early evening when we walked the rest of the way to his apartment, and the light was soft through the window, and he kissed me gently on the neck, and we lay down together on the mattress in his room. The next morning the sweepers were out with their maroon outfits, the bottom half of the legs orange as if they'd been dipped in a vat of melted traffic cones, they traversed the centers of the streets, sweeping up broken bottles and other trash, removing the evidence of the parties Roberto and I had missed the night before, calling to one another over the hard scrapes of their brooms across the pavement. It was a cold morning, there had been rain during the night, but the windows of the room were half open and we listened to them making their way along the avenues, our limbs still stacked on top of each other. Roberto's skin felt different from the skin of boys my age, his thighs were dry, paper-like, but his hands were steady, they'd moved with purpose. The joke from the hostels was finally right, it was heaven.

Roberto lived just above the Ponte Milvio, down a small ivy-filled passage I would have called a driveway but he and all of his neighbors called a "tunnel," emphasis on the first syllable so that it matched the last one of cartoon. The bars of this neighborhood spread their patrons languidly out into the streets, I came to enjoy leaving his small room in the mornings and passing through them for a cappuccino before continuing the long way back to Parioli, looping right to avoid the horrible elevated express road filled with empty beer bottles and condoms used in despair after Lazio games. His bedroom was built under a mansard roof, and the ceiling sloped down to wood-framed windows that opened out onto the tunnel, and everything out the window was green, white, or brown. In this room, with Roberto, I felt as if we'd left the oranges and pinks of the rest of the city behind.

Within a few weeks everyone in my family had met Roberto, I could see Clea especially approved, it made me more serious in her eyes and she invited us to the movies with her and Marco. Dida was so absorbed in her family, she had no special interest in Roberto except that he represented a way that I could follow her path, which she was encouraging of, she was already despairing that after four months her baby did not yet have a cousin. Roberto was especially charming with my aunts, he had a special affection for older women, and I wondered if it was because of the loss of his mother. He and Fahad would spend entire evenings in long conversations about world political events, often joined by Marco, the only thing that perplexed me was that he and Andrea did not warm to each other. There was no animosity, but this fact of their benign indifference allowed me to admit that my family was not the monolith I believed them to be, they still were able to have individual reactions and preferences, even if they were always enacted in the group setting. I saw my family so frequently now, they were already talking of teaching me to make certain holiday dishes, though it amused me that neither Clea nor Dida could cook, their mother cooked for them.

My relationships with my family had become easier, somehow. Their intensity and irony bothered me less, I was able to delight in their use of language, the demands of intimacy also seemed easier to bear. On one of our evenings together, while Settimia finished in the kitchen and Giacomo set a single bottle of wine for the nine of us to share over dinner on the table, Andrea jumped in when the conversation tilted back toward me and what kind of work I wasn't finding, now that I was back in the family fold, it seemed he regarded me as having no secrets. She is writing a book, he declared. It's about the Hebrews. I listened, amazed, as he spun out a story for everyone that I could see was totally plausible from his point of view, the few things I'd asked him about or that he'd seen me reading, that Palestinian book, the painter, I was shocked at how complete the narrative was in his own version of reality. And I realized I had two choices, I could attempt to correct Andrea's version of reality, or I could live it. So I told them about Vietri.

I myself thought my search for Vietri was so weird that I was continually surprised that the Italians I told didn't think there was anything unusual about it. There were so many mysterious rules and reasons for doing things, they were all so high-strung and uncompromising, I remembered Clea once taking the eggs out of my hands one morning at the beach when we were young and I'd wanted to make myself some scrambled eggs for breakfast. She'd returned them to their spot on the counter, eggs weren't for breakfast and so I would not be eating them. They were cosmopolitans, these Romans, still one Fourth of July they'd asked what Americans ate on this holiday and I'd described corn on the cob and they'd looked at me in horror. But it's pig food! Dida had said. Only in Rome did being cosmopolitan have absolutely no association with open-mindedness. They were all still shocked by my instinct to drink the tap water, this despite their lectures to me on the failures of American environmental policy.

You know, Marco said, there are TV shows that can do this for you, find someone, Clea was rolling her eyes, but it's true, he continued, waving his hand at her, my mother watches them, and they hire journalists, too, I have some friends who have gotten work. Clea interrupted, clearly embarrassed by Marco and wanting to take this in a more serious, factual direction. There are two television shows that are premised on finding people, she explained. *Chi l'ha visto?* is on RAI and it is about people who have gone missing. They explain the case and then they wait for people to call in with information. Lots of adopted children finding their birth parents, teenage runways, things like that. *C'è posta per te* is sillier. It's people who want to send a "letter" to someone they knew long ago, usually an old boyfriend who left them, something like that. It's very melodramatic. They actually send someone dressed like a postman to deliver the letter, like a male model, someone too attractive to really be a postman. We were all laughing, but

I was shaking my head, shocked at a world in which everyone knew my secrets. Well, Marco said, just let me know if you want to do it, my mother would love it!

Even though he had met my Roman family, I still felt that I was keeping much of myself from Roberto, I was realizing at last that the facts of my family were separate from my true self, I had told Roberto the first, but the second still felt untouched. I couldn't bring myself to ask Roberto if I was the only person he was seeing, I was aware that one answer would devastate me, and the other would trap me. I had never considered my life in Berkeley to be real, had never expected anything that happened before that great uncertainty of my life was resolved to matter, and it wasn't that my life in Rome felt more real to me, but the passage of the years since college had suggested to me that perhaps this was as real as life would ever feel. There was no secret level I would finally find, just the world and the people before me, and what I would do with them. Perhaps, I was also realizing, it wasn't only up to me to decide if my actions mattered.

I was seeing that for Dida, the rest of my cousins, their lives flowed seamlessly out of the elder generations, their place had been waiting for them in advance of their arrival. But I knew I wasn't like this, accepting my place in the family system did not give me all of the answers, I was absorbed and yet I still didn't know what to do, my cousins had never needed to reconcile multiple narrative threads. I had always wondered if my mother's schizophrenia would have developed if she had stayed in Italy, and now I wondered if her desire for a coherent story was simply a longing for the one she had left.

There had been a drought for most of my childhood in California, one that lasted a biblical seven years, and during that time, before these ideas had merged or transformed into her theories about my grandfather, my mother had become obsessed with rivers. Away from the coast as we were, those great, lazy rivers of my childhood, the American, the Russian, the Sacramento, where one could float down a gentle stream on an inner tube for days, were assumed as the image of water by the psyche. My mother began to collect maps, historical, topographical, maps of their floodplains. She ordered books from the local library, drove with me to the levees and peered down at the banks suspiciously. She developed a grand theory that all the rivers had once been one mighty river, which had carved the valley. She would sit me down, and with a desperation that embarrassed me, it should have worried me, but I was so young, it didn't worry me, it embarrassed me, she tried to explain it to me, passionately drew her fingers over the maps, tried to show me how they all had once been one great river nearly the width of the state. She'd studied chemical water treatments during her master's, she knew a lot about the science, I didn't know anything, why shouldn't I believe her? But I didn't believe her, and she cared so much, over and over she tried to make me see. When my father got home from work she'd quietly slide the maps back into the drawer and put her finger to her lips, our secret.

One year, the year before it got "very bad," my father had one of the maps framed as a Christmas gift. It was one she studied often, made at the beginning of the twentieth century, showing the current boundaries, and, almost whimsically, where the river might have spread, the other paths it might have taken. The colors of the map were oranges and golds, though it depicted water, and my father had chosen a pale cerulean for the matting, a deep redwood for the frame, I remembered it as one of the most elegant things I'd ever seen. But my mother's expression changed as she realized that her beloved map was encased away from her. She began to wail, and threw it on the floor, shattering the glass. I'd never wished more than in that moment that I'd had a sibling, someone to clutch hands with, someone in the lifeboat with me. Instead I sat stock-still as the rest of the scene played out, my father trying to comfort her, sweeping up the glass, the broken frame, later, out by the garbage. It was one of my most feared memories, worse even than the days in the motel, and I curled away from it whenever it crept on the edges of my thoughts.

Years later, when I could finally bring myself to, I would do some reading on schizophrenia. I had to do it while pretending I wasn't doing it, with eight other browser tabs open so I could click away at any moment as if burned. The line I remembered from these quick bursts of research was that schizophrenia, or maybe it was hallucinations in particular, was the brain trying to make a coherent story out of the disparate and often false and disorienting information it was receiving. In those final years while living with us, my mother had thrown all of her energy, all of her intelligence, all of her love, into this project, she cared more about proving the rivers were the same than I had ever seen anyone care about anything. I'd realized that it was no wonder my mother cared so much about this story about the river, this story was the only thing she had.

Sometimes I worried, wondering if I was any different, I was trying to assemble the facts of the world into an understanding of Vietri, instead of voices on the flat line of a motel telephone I had the massacre of monks in Ethiopia, instead of braided rivers I had a painter exiled to a town of white clay, I was attempting to exchange those days in the motel with a man who'd once ordered hundreds of scholarly books on every topic from a bookstore in Berkeley. I had a feeling of grasping, that if I could only sift together all of the stories I had heard, if I could understand these stories as a part of one story, maybe, maybe I would get close. I wondered if I was trying to save myself, and I wondered if it would work.

Chapter Eighteen

It turned out that Roberto did not live far from Vietri's apartment. The streets to the via Bevanda sloped up from the river, turning at ninety-degree angles, and one Saturday morning I walked up them, passing a mother in a yellow coat and heeled boots loading her toddler into a car, several elderly couples out for walks, an Asian man crouched alone on the sidewalk with an assortment of alarm clocks, scissors, various other small practical things for sale. A young African man stood in front of the café where I'd taken the Palestinian book from the unknown Chiara and told me buongiorno formally, as if it were his one line in a play. Earlier, when walking up the hill, a man with white hair behind the wheel of a small car had slowed almost to a stop and waved at me, smiling as if I were known and dear to him.

Potted plants, trees, ropes of ivy were everywhere around me, as they were everywhere in Rome. In Parioli the ivy was protective, sometimes even plastic, threaded through wooden gates and chain-link fences to obscure both the view of the inside and the fact of its concealing. Here the abundance felt natural, part of the buildings, the sidewalks, the balconies themselves. I walked to Vietri's apartment that morning, but, standing before the gate, I didn't ring the buzzer. Exhaling, I realized that this was no longer what I was after. It wasn't that I didn't want to know, didn't want to meet him, but it was the same way that I'd stopped checking my ex-boyfriend's Facebook page, though I felt regret I hadn't before, I now had no desire to analyze pictures taken at house parties for which girls were trying to sleep with him, I had at last absorbed some lesson that freed me from the actual person. Vietri was no longer just one person, finding him, talking to him, asking him questions, this was no longer what I wanted, to understand him I would need to absorb something more complicated, something enormous, perhaps encompassing a century of this country's history, or my own.

Instead I decided to go to Aliano. I wanted to see the town in which Vietri had been born, where the painter had spent his two lonely years, though I no longer thought I would meet Vietri I was beginning to conclude that there was importance in the past and its landscapes. I'd taken a train from Rome that morning, waking up at four, had transferred buses twice. My second bus pulled into Aliano around five o'clock, and in the evening light the town was a dusty yellow-gray. I knew it had been mostly destroyed by an earthquake in the '80s, and some buildings sat open still, three walls supported by neighboring houses, stone guts spilling out into the road. Dozens of old men lined the street in front of the church like crows on a wire, observing all as I descended the bus, the church bell going at unsettlingly irregular intervals. I went to the only open business to buy a water and before me a young man ordered a café and a prosecco, he sipped the espresso and an old man whose front row of teeth had been ground down into nothing appeared and drank down the cup of prosecco in four unsteady sips. I left the bar and went to look for the room I'd booked online on the Street of Hungarian Martyrs, and at first no one answered, but after some minutes a man appeared from behind me in the street, he must have been watching me, and exchanged my passport for a room key. When I got into the room, I lay on the bed, suddenly exhausted.

After an hour or so I got up and wandered the town in the fading light, took a walk down the large hill. The landscape was disorienting, from one view you saw only the strange white formations of the calanchi rising lunar and ghostly, like the Badlands in South Dakota, but from the other side of the town you saw only the green cultivated fields of the valley, a perfect snowcapped Apennine peak beyond. The old part of the town, the part where the painter had stayed, was at the bottom, the ravine steep beyond it.

I had told Loredana I was taking a short trip, but I didn't want to announce my departure more broadly. Was I intentionally testing Roberto? That night, seeing the messages I'd received from him throughout the day, I called him and explained where I was. Ah, he said. I said I wasn't sure how long I would stay. Okay, he said. Well, I hope you will tell me when you come back to Rome. Of course I will, I said, surprised at his plaintive tone. Of course.

The next morning I asked the lady who'd appeared to set out yogurt and coffee in the shared kitchen about a family

with the name of Vietri, and she shrugged and said the old
man would know, but didn't tell me how to find the old man.
I spent the day walking through the hills, eating dinner at the
small restaurant attached to my hotel, served four courses
alone in the menuless restaurant despite my protestations. No
one had heard of a family with the surname Vietri. The painter
was a tourist attraction for them, no one who remembered him
as a person had been alive for twenty years. I pressed the yogurt woman, who was running the restaurant as well, and she
said the old man was away, maybe he'd be back in a week or
two, maybe a month, he was visiting his daughter, there was
no way to tell with these things, I could wait if I wanted.

On the day I decided to return to Rome, I climbed to the graveyard at the top of the hill, the graveyard where the painter had
wanted to be buried, and at its edge I looked down across the
valley. The hills from this view were striated, blanched white.
There were two tiers, one farther down the hill where the
gravestones were older, some of them toppled or cracked. I
wandered there, up and down the rows, reading the names,
the dates of birth and death, occasionally phrases in Latin or
small etchings of angels or crests, the distances between the
years impressively long or achingly short. It was in a far corner
that I found it, the gravestone that read "Maddalena Vietri, b.
1901, d. 1945." I remembered her name from the military records, I slipped down to my knees in front of the grave, resting
my weight on the backs of my feet, this was Vietri's mother.

The grave was well tended, free of weeds or overgrowth, the stone was weathered but had no cracks. I searched the rows around it several times, but could find no other Vietri gravestones, she was alone. And when she died, Vietri would have been twenty-five.

What else did I need to know about Vietri? He would have grown up in this village of bone-white clay and short shadows, would have spent his childhood in the dust, with half of his fellow children dead before their fifth year, where he either had or had not befriended a painter already marked for death. He'd wanted to go to Africa or he hadn't, but either way he'd gone there as part of an army, he would have had no skills, nothing to offer, just young bones, had some job given to the most expendable, say a motorcycle driver, an easy target for the planes and snipers along the uncovered desert roads. Then the ships would have stopped arriving, there would have been no water, he would have waited with his fellow soldiers while bombs dropped and men disappeared into flames and sand, sometimes without a trace of blood, the nights would have been cold and long and what would there have been to do but talk, like so many of his generation he would have learned Italian in the army, wrenching his soft voice from the swamp of his dialect toward a common vocabulary, and maybe there were men there on those nights who would have been in Ethiopia, and maybe they would have had stories, or photographs they called trophies, and new stories would have been a rarity, and maybe there was a man who'd spoken of the monastery and the shallow gulley where they'd thrown the bodies of the monks, and if he had heard this story, he, a boy who had grown up praying to a black Madonna, what would he have thought of this massacre of black Christians? He would have been at El Alamein, would have taken part in a battle for an expanse of Libyan desert that was today still under conflict, sent to a trench that faced that other army across a patch of desert, in front of them would have been mines and snipers, behind them desert, Germans, and when the British overran them they would have surrendered with exhaustion that was something like cheerfulness. He would have spent weeks in the impromptu prison camps set up in the desert, and then onto a boat, with fresh water at last, tinny, and strictly rationed, but fresh, and the caps of waves in the sea would have been like shark fins, but the real fear would have been torpedoes, and yet torpedoes, for a boy who would have seen his first car at the age of nine, who wouldn't have used a toilet with running water until he arrived in Ravenna for the army, how could he have been scared of a torpedo, in what world did these things coexist? The British officers on the ship would have treated them like children, with disdain, belowdecks with them would have been Indians and Chinese, the cooks, the cleaners, not in the same spaces, but he would have heard, sometimes, strange other languages, he who would have never met even a German before Africa. He would have been a prisoner of war in a foreign land, most likely England, farming alongside the rural women of the countryside, wearing great brown coveralls they called tutas with large yellow circles on their backs, roaming from farm to farm, repeating the cycle, this would have been his life for almost six years, when they arrived in England America would have had yet to enter the war. It would have been where he had learned English, maybe he'd been lodged in a country house with an enormous library, maybe there'd been a local he'd befriended, either way there had been lots of time, years and years in that green damp country. After his third year, things would have changed, away in the war, the Italian king had begun a speech to a friend, "My dear duce, it is no longer any good," and the Americans had prepared an invasion of the peninsula, and the princess of Italy, married to the grandson of a German emperor, was arrested while attending the funeral of her brother-in-law, the king of Bulgaria, and, on the day the laborers in England observed the harvest festival, as these formerly enemy soldiers celebrated the end of the season's work having affirmed that they had no allegiance to that party of a duce that no longer existed, the Italian princess, mother of four, was sent to the concentration camp at Buchenwald, where she was to bleed to death short months later after the amputation of her right arm, wounded during the bombing of a munitions factory. And in the north, the painter would have waited in a town overlooking a lake made by an enormous, long-melted glacier, wondering if he and his family would be permitted across a border. That would have been two years before the war would end, but it would be another year after that before Vietri would be repatriated, and in that time he would have turned twenty-five, still away from home, and his mother had died, her child still far from her.

And then? Repatriated at last, say that he would have gone to Rome instead of returning to his motherless town, would have gotten a job, probably as a laborer of some sort, depending on who he'd befriended in the POW camp, years would have passed. Then somehow he would have been involved in that trial in the '80s, I would never know what he'd seen, what he'd done, I would never know what blood was on his hands, whether he'd washed it away, but he'd survived the years of lead, his years had continued, he had survived. Maybe he'd had a chance encounter with the American women who'd founded the pottery company, maybe they'd known they needed someone with connections with laborers or at the ports, maybe they'd taken his name as a sign. And maybe it would have been enough to extract himself from whatever structures of favors had ensnared him in the trial, enough to start a new story, one in which he was an elderly man who ordered esoteric academic books in English from a bookstore in California. And in all this time, would he have thought of the monks in Ethiopia, if he knew of them, or would he have thought of the things he witnessed himself during the war that I would never know? Maybe the orders of the books were an atonement, maybe they were a project Casaubon, but either way, did it matter? It didn't even matter if he read all of the books, they were there, and when he wanted to read them he would read them. And when he didn't read them they would have been there for him as well.

When I'd arrived in Rome I had wanted to walk into a room filled with dusty book light and find Vietri in a low chair, I had wanted to sit on a stool at his feet like an acolyte and have him tell me everything he'd learned from his books, that is, I had wanted him to tell me how I should live this life. But I knew now that this was as close to Vietri as I would get, and as I inhaled the warm air, felt the tip of my nose begin to burn, as I rose from the grave site, I thought that maybe it would be enough.

An image arose of my parents in California, I pictured them side by side for the first time in years. In Rome there was Loredana with her fragile heart, Andrea, Dida, Settimia, they were a net that would hold me, and Roberto was waiting for me, steady and deep. I had been going through my life as if all of our circles didn't touch, but they did, if not interlocking exactly, then the membranes were thin, they bumped and they merged. But I could see now that though Vietri's circle and mine had met, they would no longer, our arcs branched out from here, to force anything else would be counter to the great pattern I could see had always been at work beneath our feet. Where his arc had gone I didn't know, I knew now I would never know, but I saw more clearly where mine could go, I could arc, gloriously, back to Rome, or to California, I had my aunts and my cousins, and Roberto's circle, mine, they could come together, at least for a while. When he was twenty-five, Vietri had lost his mother, but I still had my mother, she was still alive, and even if she couldn't change I now knew that I could.

I descended the road from the graveyard and the valley laid itself out greenly before me. I packed my bag in the small, stone room, reclaimed my passport from the man at the desk, and when the bus arrived I boarded it back toward Rome. I curled my feet underneath me on the seat, embraced my knees to my chest, let my forehead rest against the window to absorb the southern light, patient and strong. And then? What was this life, if I could have it, to be?

Acknowledgments

I owe an enormous debt of gratitude to many for their support of this novel. Thank you:

To my agent, Julie Barer, for her considered readings and expert guidance—it's been a dream. To Nicole Cunningham, everyone at The Book Group, and to Jenny Meyer and Caspian Dennis.

To my editor, Mary Gaule, whose faith, sharp mind, and enthusiasm have been a joy. To everyone at Harper, including Nikki Baldauf, Jocelyn Larnick, Cindy Achar, Joanne O'Neill, Kristin Cipolla, and Erin Kibby.

To Chrissy Hennessey and Anu Jindal, first readers.

To the Center for Fiction, whose fellowship arrived at the right moment, especially to Noreen Tomassi and Sara Batkie. To Patricia Mulcahy, whose early editorial eye was invaluable. And to my fellow fellows, Lisa Chen, t'ai freedom ford, Melissa Rivero, Samantha Storey, and Ruchika Tomar.

To the UNCW MFA program, Robert Anthony Siegel, and especially Rebecca Lee. To Erica Sklar, Lucy Huber, Katie Jones, Sally Johnson, Ana Alvarez, and Carson Vaughan.

To everyone I worked with at *Ecotone* and Lookout Books, particularly Anna Lena Phillips Bell, Emily Louise Smith, David Gessner, Beth Staples, and Ben George.

To *Agni* and *Joyland,* for their early support of my work.

To Rochelle Davis and her book *Palestinian Village Histories*, the authors of *Suhmata*, and the work of Carlo Levi. To Briana Kobor for her honeymoon.

To Karen and Bill McClung, Christina Creveling, Sorayya Carr, and Rose Barreto.

To Sarah Phair, Alexa Stark, and Meredith Miller, for work advice and book advice.

To Blakely Simoneau.

To my family. I got very lucky. Especially to my sisters Natalya and Stacy, my Uncle Rick and Aunt Genell, and my parents, John Theye and Michelle DeRobertis.

To Salvatore.

About the Author

NICOLA DEROBERTIS-THEYE was an Emerging Writing Fellow at the New York Center for Fiction, and her work has been published in *Agni*, *Electric Literature*, and *LitHub*. A graduate of UC Berkeley, she received an MFA in Creative Nonfiction from the University of North Carolina, Wilmington, where she was the fiction editor for the literary magazine *Ecotone*. She is a native of Oakland, California, and lives in Brooklyn, New York.